Footprints ∮[To]∮ Nowhere

A Novel By

Robert S. Armstrong

This is a work of fiction. All of the characters,
organizations, and events portrayed in this novel
are either products of the author's imagination
or are used fictitiously.

ISBN: 1468145746
ISBN-13: 978-1468145748

ACKNOWLEDGMENTS

I would like to thank Robert Kirchenbauer for his support and assistance in writing this book. I also wish to thank Kathy Kemp, Sheriff Jerry Colson and Mary Conway for providing background information essential to the story.

This book is dedicated to my wife, Nanci who provided her time proof reading, her insights, support and encouragement.

PROLOGUE

Patrolman Larry Sizemore headed down Route I-80 traveling west from his home in Laramie. As a member of the Wyoming State Patrol, he usually made the trip in this area as part of his regular routine. It was cold, not unusual for November. In the fall there were chilly temperatures, thirty to forty degrees. It was colder at night. As he continued towards Arlington, a light snow was falling and the powder dusted his two lanes of the four lane highway as he drove. The white flakes blew on the black hood of his car and skimmed the windshield. As he approached Arlington, the highway led him down an incline and Elk Mountain stood before him. Pine trees lined the landscape standing before a sheer cliff at the base of the lush, green mountain. Light patches of snow mixed with brown areas speckled the mountainside.

Continuing on, he passed the Wagonhound Road exit sign and spotted a van parked on the exit ramp to his right. It was parked on the shoulder of the ramp facing the rest area beyond. The van was facing away from Elk Mountain which stood imposingly in the background.

He recognized the Chevy model which was too elaborate to belong to someone from these parts. The driver's side door was open, the keys were in the ignition and the motor was still running. Sizemore pulled his black and white patrol car up behind it and cautiously got out. He put on his tan flat brimmed hat and got out of the car and closed the white-sided door. Light flakes of snow fell on his head and green jacket. As he approached, he noticed the Maryland tags on the back and noticed a small dent in the back fender. Otherwise, the van appeared brand new. Getting closer, he heard music which he recognized as the Steve Miller Band. Guitars and an organ played and voices sang in harmony.

He approached the driver's side and peered inside. The music was coming from the radio. There was an open red and white cooler on the passenger's side seat and an opened orange juice carton sat in the cooler. A few granola bar wrappers and an open package of beef jerky lay on the console and on the floor of the passenger's side.

The puzzled patrolman perused the barren landscape looking for any sign of the driver. Where could he have gone?

Snow covered the steep shoulder of the road and the high grass beyond. Dispersed along the rocky landscape, shrubs poked through, trying to survive the unforgiving terrain. There was no sign of the driver except footprints in the snow leading across the plains towards the horizon.

CHAPTER ONE

Don was a popular guy.

The year was 1963. John Kennedy was president and Vietnam was on the horizon. The gym was full of high school students; banners of KENDALL FOR PRESIDENT were everywhere. Paper banners were pasted on the wall behind the podium displaying the names of the candidates in red. The place was alive with enthusiasm and the students anticipated the speeches. There was the faint rumble of talking and a smattering of laughter.

The candidates were on a small platform in the brand new gym which had bleachers on each side populated with students. A shiny floor was lined with folding chairs holding students and teachers.

Don was clean cut with a broad smile and short light brown hair, combed back with a wave in front. He had an athletic build and was of medium height. He wore a dark blue sport coat a button down white shirt and a striped tie. His alert blue eyes scanned the audience as he spoke at the podium.

It was hard not to be impressed by Don's manner and speech. For his sixteen years he appeared and acted more mature than the other kids in attendance. He had ambition, plans and was going somewhere. Even though he was clearly superior to many others his age, he was friendly and unassuming. Don's voice was strong and impressive. Not too high or low, just even. The students loudly applauded, convinced that he was their choice.

After the assembly was over and leaving the gym, Don walked past his sister, Kathy.

"Hey sis" he greeted, as Don walked along with her out of the gym.

"How was my speech?" Don asked.

"I was convinced you are the greatest… even though you are my brother," she kidded.

The Kendalls lived back off a well traveled road in middle class suburban Baltimore County Maryland, just over the city line. The area was residential with mostly older individual homes and some new construction. The Woodlawn area was typically suburban— houses spread apart with patches of woods. Their brown shingled frame house sat back down a dusty gravel driveway on two acres of property. There was a fenced in field where a barn stood near the house. The family had two horses and was fond of horseback riding. Don's horse, a black and white pinto, was named Traveler, after Robert E. Lee's.

Don and Kathy were very close growing up, especially after their parent's divorce two years ago. Kathy was just over a year younger. As children, they would have fun fantasizing about finding the Loch Ness monster and Big Foot. The two of them shared and interest in the Civil War, reading and talking about it.

Kathy had that infectious Kendall smile, shoulder length blond hair, crystal blue eyes and a pretty face.

"Do you think I will win the election?"

"Are you kidding? They love you."

"I think there are big things in your future," she said, smiling. The two walked down the locker lined hall to class.

Mr. Charles Shepard was one of the most popular Social Studies teachers at Woodlawn. He was about twenty-five, somewhat stocky in build with rounded, muscular shoulders and short cut brown hair parted on the side. This quarter they were studying the Civil War. Don had been fascinated with Abraham Lincoln since childhood. He found the life of Lincoln a great inspiration as well as his role in the Civil War. As a child, he often played trivia games with Kathy.

"Today we will be discussing Lincoln's assassination on April fifteenth, eighteen sixty-five," Mr. Shepard announced sitting down at his office style desk in the front of the classroom.

"How many of you know who the assassin was?"

Most of the class raised their hand.

"It is well known that his name was John Wilkes Booth."

Confident that Don knew the entire story, Mr. Shepard directed his question to him.

"Don, can you tell us what happened that day?"

"Mr. Shepard, I think I can give the class an idea of what happened," Don said modestly. The members of the class knowingly smiled. They were quite aware of Don's fascination with Lincoln. Don paused slightly before continuing.

"John Wilkes Booth was sympathetic to the Confederacy in the Civil War and he hated Lincoln for his harsh wartime policies. He and his co-conspirators couldn't accept that they had lost the war and wanted revenge. Booth plotted with three others to kidnap Lincoln and was motivated to become a hero of the south. Booth wanted to kill Lincoln after the plan to abduct him failed. He was able to gain entry to Ford's Theatre that evening due to his fame as an actor. In his day he was like a movie star. Everyone at the theatre knew him. The president's bodyguard was elsewhere in the theatre. Booth peered through a hole in the door of the theatre viewing box where the president and his wife were sitting to see exactly where the president was. In addition to Mrs. Lincoln, there was another couple sharing the presidential booth of the theatre. Booth walked up behind the president, took out a small gun and shot him on the side of the head at point blank range. Booth then jumped from the President's box onto the stage. He shouted Sic simper tyrannis."

"Which means, thus it shall ever be for tyrants," Mr. Shepard added.

"He caught his foot on draping material and landed awkwardly. When he landed, he broke his leg. His adrenaline was high and he kept running out the side door even though he was injured. The stage manager tried to stop him and Booth cut him with a knife. The audience sat in stunned silence as Booth got away. Booth had a horse waiting outside the theater for a quick getaway. He got on and headed south with his co-conspirator, David Herold to Sarattsville, in Prince George's County. He stopped where Mary Saratt used to live, a boarding house and tavern. He picked up a few supplies including rifles, rope and field glasses which were reportedly left there after the kidnapping attempt and continued to ride south towards Virginia."

"Thank you Don." Mr. Shepard got up, stood by the blackboard and continued the story.

Intrigued, the class listened intently.

"Booth's next stop was Dr. Samuel Mudd's farm, further south of Washington. Booth knew Mudd because he was once introduced by a confederate spy. Mudd treated Booth's broken leg and with federal troops pursuing them, the two men continued to ride south to the Cox home where they hid in a thicket. They crossed the Potomac River into Northern Virginia, eventually stopping at the Garrett farm where troops caught up with them. They hid in a tobacco barn on the property. They were asked to surrender and Herold decided to give himself up. Booth was shot in the back of the neck and he died at a farmhouse nearby. There were four people eventually hanged for their role in the kidnapping and assassination: George Atzerodt, who lost his nerve when attempting to kill Vice President Andrew Johnson, Lewis Paine, who attempted to stab the Secretary of State, William Seward that day, David Herold and Mary Saratt. Mudd and Cox were charged in aiding the assassins. Mary Saratt was the first woman ever hanged in the United States. There was some question about whether Mary Saratt was directly involved and deserved to die. Does the class have any opinions about Mary or the other conspirators?"

Susan, another member of the class raised her hand and spoke up. "I think that Mary Saratt was guilty. She did own a boarding house in Washington where planning for the kidnapping took place and I think Mary knew about it."

A different classmate, Gene, agreed. "She also still owned the tavern and boarding house where discussions were held and items were stored for Booth to pick up after his escape."

Mr. Shepard remained neutral.

"What do you think Don?"

He disagreed with the others. Don wondered if the federal government had gotten it right.

"I have my doubts about Mary Saratt's guilt in the assassination of Lincoln and the circumstantial evidence linking her to the kidnapping."

Later in 1963, Don won the election for class president of Woodlawn Senior High School. He graduated in 1965 and would be on his way to bigger and better things. That year, Kathy would never have imagined that Don would one day mysteriously disappear.

CHAPTER TWO

Eleven years later, Don lived in New York City. He had grad-uated from Lehigh University with a degree in Business Administration and History. While at Lehigh, he was the president of his fraternity. His interest in the Civil War had continued since high school. He was the vice president of the Lincoln Society of New York. He now worked for a large advertising firm on Madison Avenue. He was an up-and-coming advertising executive for Klein and Associates. His office was in a forty story, modern glass struc-ture. The busy street was a mixture of office buildings, high end retail stores, and upscale galleries. The wall of windows gleamed in the sunlight as he approached the set of entrance doors. Down the street he could see the late summer trees in Central Park beyond Fifth Avenue.

He entered the large lobby and approached the elevator. He was wearing a gray pinstriped, three piece Brooks Brother's suit accentuated by a lavender tie. He had grown a light brown mus-tache since high school. As Don got on, a co-worker stepped on just behind him. Over the last two years he had made friends and was especially chummy with Judith, a fellow executive.

"Hi Judith," Don said after she got on.

"Are you doing anything this weekend?"

"Yeah, I'm going to a party," she replied.

Judith DePetro had worked on Madison Avenue for thirteen years. She was ambitious but as a woman, there was certain hesitancy in a man's world to promote her. As a result, she hadn't achieved the status Don had attained. She was resentful but accepting of her role in the firm. Judith was a tall, shapely woman a few years older than Don. Her Italian lineage evident, she was attractive but not Don's type. She had on a form fitting dress of a conservative blue color and a colorful scarf around her neck.

Her dark brown hair was tied up in a bun. Judith was very fond of Don and felt there could have been more than just a friendship. If she got the least bit of encouragement, she would show her deeper feelings toward him.

Don was a regular attendee of parties, but he hadn't done anything socially for a while. "This party is at a friend's apartment in the West Village. Are you interested?"

"Sure, it might be fun," Don said with an interested look.

"I'll call you about seven and we can make plans."

"Okay," Don said with enthusiasm.

Don got off the elevator on the twelfth floor and walked to his office. He entered the suite and walked past his secretary's desk. Paulette was not there and apparently had gone on an errand. As he entered the spacious office the phone rang. He quickly grabbed the receiver putting his brief case down.

"Hello," Don answered.

"Hi Donny."

"Hi Sis!" Don was pleased to hear from her. He hadn't talked to her for two months.

"How are you?" Don said as he sat down at his desk in the plush leather chair.

"I'm doing great! Things are good here in Woodbine. Don's sister had since gotten married and was living in Carroll County, Maryland.

"I'm doing well," Don responded.

"I made a presentation to a large corporate client and got the account."

"Great," Kathy said. "You have done very well."

"Hey listen. I was wondering... do you want to go on a trip with me to Gettysburg to look for Lincoln memorabilia?"

"Okay, that sounds interesting. When do you want to go? I'll be available for a weekend in a few weeks. I'll call you to confirm," Don told her.

"Okay Donny, I will look for your call."

"Okay Kathy, I love you. Bye."

"I love you too. Bye Donny."

It was then that Paulette returned and entered the office. She had been working at Klein for five years and was good friends with Don.

"Hey Paulette, do you want to go to a party with Judith and I tonight?"

Paulette was a perky blond and reminded Don of his sister. She was always cheerful and was the life of the office.

"Sorry Don, I have other plans. I have a hot date tonight."

"Okay... maybe next time," Don said, looking a little disappointed.

That evening the two arrived at the apartment of Judith's acquaintance. They were on a small street with trees lining the sidewalk. It was a small walk up in a row of older houses, each having a set of steps and a small porch leading to the large glass archway door. As he approached the house, Don thought that back home in Baltimore, they called them row houses. They walked into the living room and the party was crowded with people, mostly their age. The host was introduced by Judith.

"Robert this is Don."

"Hi," the host said to Don with a slurred, alcohol induced greeting as he walked away.

Don got himself a mixed drink and wandered around the party. He was still thinking about the phone call he had received earlier in the day. He was looking forward to seeing Kathy and going on an interesting artifact trip as they had done other times.

The stereo was playing in the background. He could hear the high pitched whiney voice of Neil Young and recognized the stanzas of *Cinnamon Girl*. The sweet and pungent smell of marijuana wafted in the air. He came to a small adjoining room where there were some people sitting in a group. They were laughing and looking quite happy.

He noticed a woman holding a drink and talking with another guy. She was stunning. He had seen many beautiful women since coming to New York but he could not take his eyes off her. Her hair was light brown, long and straight to mid-back. Her blue-green eyes danced as she talked, meeting his in apparent interest. She had a model's face but her body was voluptuous, not the gaunt look of many models. Don decided to introduce himself, ignoring the man she was talking to.

"Hello," Don said.

"My name is Don." The woman looked interested and the other guy a little peeved.

"Mine is Marna," she replied with a smile. She extended her hand and Don gently grasped hers and shook it.

"Are you from New York?"

"No, New Jersey."

"New Jersey? That's not really a state is it?" Don joked. Marna chuckled at the attempt. The other guy standing there became uncomfortable. Left out of the conversation, he walked away.

Don was never a ladies man although easy with people. After starting a conversation with a woman he became self conscious and the conversation became awkward. It seemed that when he did get involved in a relationship he could not open himself to it. This was a very natural feeling. It was going well. The positive vibes were there. It was as if they had known each other for years.

"I'm from Maryland...Baltimore."

"Well Marna, this is a nice party. I don't get to Greenwich Village often," Don said, trying to make conversation. He still couldn't believe her considerable interest in him.

"Don, do you work in New York."

"Yes, on Madison Avenue at Klein."

"Oh really, I have a friend who is working in advertising."

"What a coincidence," Don commented.

"How about you?" Don asked. "Where do you work?"

"Right now I'm waiting tables at a restaurant here in the East Village."

"Oh really? ... which restaurant?"

She is really great! She's beautiful!, Don thought. *I have to get her number.*

"A little place near Washington Square called Minnelli's."

"I guess the commute is pretty long to the city."

"I don't live in Jersey, I grew up there. Now my apartment is in Chelsea."

It was then that Judith came into the room.

"Don, do you mind if we leave? I'm getting kind of bored."

"Okay, I guess."

Don introduced the two. "This is Marna. That's Judith."

Don gave her a knowing look. "Give me a few minutes."

Judith walked over to the other side of the room, mixing with the crowd.

"Marna I would like to get your number." Don said with confidence.

"Sure."

She wrote it down with a pen from her purse.

CHAPTER THREE

Don lived in an apartment in Midtown Manhattan, thirteen blocks down Fifth Avenue from his office. He had a condo in a large building at One-Sixty Central Park. It was a forty-story, tan, squarish multilevel art deco building with roof top terrace gardens. The Essex House was built in nineteen-thirty with a grand view of Central Park. It sat among other, more modern skyscrapers. As Don approached, the flags mounted on the wall in front of the building were gently moving in the summer breeze. It was pleasant and cool as the sun was setting. The luxury apartment building had several wide entrance doors trimmed with brass. The doorman greeted him and opened the door.

Don thought about Marna at the party last evening. How wonderful the feeling had been when talking to her. He looked forward to calling her.

The apartment was a one bedroom, certainly within Don's price range. It was decorated with modern, stylish furniture. Don walked in, flopped down on the couch removed his suit coat, and loosened his tie. It had been a long day at work. He mixed himself a drink and picked up the phone to call Marna, reading the number off the matchbook she gave him. It was about seven-thirty. He wasn't sure if she was working that shift and would be home. The phone rang a couple times and she answered.

"Hello." Marna's voice was familiar but different over the phone.

"Hello, this is Don Kendall."

"Hi Don, I was hoping you would call."

"I've been looking forward to talking to you too."

Don was pleased that she had been thinking about him. He decided to just get to the point. He felt good about the rapport.

"I was wondering if we could get together on Friday night."

"Sure, I would like that."

"I thought we could go to a restaurant for dinner, and possibly a club."

Don was not sure about his choice but was sure she would be interested in most things he suggested.

"I'll pick you up at six."

"Okay, see you then."

"Wait! Let me get your address," Don said, almost forgetting to ask her.

Don spent the rest of the week at work looking forward to his date with Marna. He saw Judith at work in the employee lounge and told her about his good conversation with Marna and the upcoming date. She felt that although she was very attractive and personable but had some reservations about her. She thought that he didn't know much about her and sensed an unpredictable quality about Marna. Don didn't care.

The following Friday evening Don took a Checker Cab to Marna's apartment in Chelsea. She lived on a busy street on the tenth floor of an apartment building near the meatpacking district. The building was generally non-descript and of faded red brick but newer than the historic brownstones of the area. The cab pulled up to the front. There were parked cars lining each side of the street. Don went to the front door and Marna stood in the entryway waiting for him. Don was surprised to see her there as he was expecting to go up to the apartment to pick her up. He got out and opened the back door of the cab.

"Hi Marna." Don smiled as he greeted her and she smiled as well.

Marna was exquisitely dressed in an off white chiffon dress which was above the knee revealing her shapely legs. She wore large diamond studded pierced earrings. She had on black velvet platform heels. Don couldn't help but think this was and expensive wardrobe on a waitress salary.

"Hello Don... Where are we headed?"

"Please call me Donny," Don insisted.

"Okay, Donny," Marna said smiling.

"I thought we might enjoy the Peacock Alley Restaurant."

"That sounds interesting. I haven't heard of it."

"It's a nice place. I'm sure you will like it," Don said encouragingly.

The cab took off down the street. Don noticed another parked car behind them pull out at the same time.

Don and Marna arrived at the Peacock Alley on Park Avenue. The restaurant was of modern elegant décor. The table Don had reservations for was at the right side of the room. The tables were set with fine white linen table cloths and each place setting had crystal goblets with fine china and ornate silverware. A candle enclosed in a glass holder sat in the middle of each table. At the far end of the room was the bar and to the right, the wall was painted with a colorful peacock mural. The couple was seated by a courteous hostess and given their menus. The two ordered vodka martinis.

Don sat across from Marna and marveled at her stunning beauty. She had the most beautiful large blue-green eyes and high cheek bones. The candle flickered with a faint glow. Her fair, blushed complexion was flawless. Her dress, which was low cut, revealed her cleavage. Don guessed that she was about twenty-five, a few years younger than he.

During dinner the conversation there were no awkward moments as Don had encountered with other beautiful women when first going out. She was a great conversationalist, intelligent and witty. She smiled often and laughed easily.

"Marna, where in New Jersey are you from?" Don asked as he sipped on his martini. Marna began to reflect back to her time growing up.

"In Vineland ... a place out in the country. I lived in a house surrounded by farmland. There are still a lot of farms out there with fields of blueberries and cantaloupes. It was a nice place to grow up. My folks and two younger brothers still live there. I came to New York to attend Columbia."

"Oh Really?"

As far as Don knew she was a beautiful waitress.

"What did you study there?"

"Well, business. I graduated and took a job on Wall Street."

"Wall Street, that's interesting, what did you do there?"

Marna began to look tense. She paused and took a few sips of her drink. Don was eager to know more about Marna and hadn't realized he was pumping her for information.

"I was a sales associate for about a year. Don, I really couldn't take that pace… the stress. I decided that I needed to think things over as far as a career choice."

Don backed off, accepted the explanation but wondered about the dramatic change of occupations.

"Don't you miss working on Wall Street? It's quite exciting. I don't know how you get by as a waitress."

"I do quite well on tips," Marna said, looking irritated.

Don dropped the issue.

After dinner as they left the restaurant as Don hailed a he noticed the same dark colored sedan across the street.

"Marna, did you see that car outside your apartment?"

"Don, "I don't think it is the same car. Are you sure?"

"Yes I think it's the same car."

"Donny, I think it is just a coincidence."

"Well… I guess so," Don reluctantly agreed.

On Monday morning Don headed to the office. When he arrived he greeted Paulette and told her about the party. His thoughts of the weekend were still fresh in his mind. He later saw Judith and recounted the wonderful but strange weekend. Judith was pleased about Don's wonderful night with Marna but was concerned about the suspicious events.

After going out to dinner again and a Broadway show the following week, Marna suggested they go out to a night club. Don decided that he was not in the mood for a club this evening and suggested they go to his apartment for drinks. After they got settled in, Don took of his suit coat and loosened his tie to relax. Marna slipped off her shoes. Don offered her a drink and he made two vodka martinis. They sat down on the couch close to each other. He embraced her in his arms and they deeply kissed. Don's nostrils sucked in her sweet exquisite scent as he breathed deeply. Don began to feel himself stirring. She was getting excited, her breath hot and quickening. Don was strangely drawn to her. Of course he wanted her sexually but he couldn't explain this unusual closeness to her. Without speaking, Don took her hand and led her to the bedroom. They slowly stripped off each other's clothes and took their time. Hot breathing and moans of pleasure were heard in the bedroom as they joined together in a rapture neither had ever experienced.

The next day Don dropped Marna off at her apartment. The two of them felt closeness as they held hands in the cab. He went up to the tenth floor on the elevator with her. They walked down a well lit but somewhat dingy hall. The walls were a faded yellow and looked as if they had not been painted for a long time. They stopped at her apartment door, number 1008.

"Marna, I will call you," Don said gazing into her eyes.

"Okay.... I really enjoyed being with you." Marna smiled, looking pleased.

They embraced and kissed deeply. Don left as she closed the apartment door.

Don returned to his apartment in the cab. The bright sun glinted off the windshields of the oncoming cars as they passed. His thoughts reflected back on the previous evening and he felt elated about his relationship with Marna. As the cab proceeded down Fifth Avenue, he again noticed the dark blue sedan which he now recognized as a Ford Crown Victoria.

The Crown Victoria, a full sized, practical sedan frequently used by law enforcement. The Ford Motor Company had been quite successful in making this car a part of mainstream Americana in the sixties. The car was often portrayed in episodes of The FBI. Ephraim Zimbalist Jr. would pursue felons in this impressive but humble conveyance. A three hundred forty- five horsepower, eight-cylinder, twin-carbarrel engine was unfairly superior to imported models with their small engines, which one could imagine were powered by a team of mice on treadmills. At least they were good on gas.

Don got off the elevator of his apartment building. As he opened the door and entered the living room the phone rang and he quickly grabbed the receiver.

"Hello," Don answered.

"How ya' doin'," a voice queried.

"Who is this?"

"Somebody you should remember." The voice did not sound familiar at all to Don. It was male and baritone. It had a taut quality. The tension was palpable.

"You ought to be careful seeing her…something might happen to you," the voice threatened.

Don was beginning to worry. W-wy?"

"Think about it… you know."

Don heard a click and a dial tone. The voice had hung up. Don wondered how this person got his phone number and even if the call was intended for him. After all, his name wasn't mentioned. It was obviously a threat… but by whom?

CHAPTER FOUR

In the coming months Don's relationship with Marna blossomed. They spent much time together. There were dinner dates at various upscale restaurants and even an Italian place in Marna's neighborhood of Chelsea. If they were being followed they didn't notice.

They spent weekend days at Central Park watching summer end and the colorful autumn leaves drop in a brilliant mix of reds, yellows and browns. Don was as happy has he had been in a long time. They would stroll around the lake holding each other, observing the waterfowl as they swam. Other walkers would throw bread in the water and watch as the ducks fought for pieces, gobbling up as many as they found.

As the leaves fell, the lovers would scoop them up. Don would pull Marna down after chasing her, embracing for a long kiss.

As they became closer, Marna revealed that she had a relationship with a stockbroker named John Weaver while she worked on Wall Street. During that time, he revealed the corrupt nature of many of the trading deals he made. He told her of an illegal multimillion dollar trade that he was about to make involving other firms. The guy felt guilty and had second thoughts about the illegal trades but was in too deep to change his mind. It was then that she learned that Dan Blackman, an exec on Madison Avenue was involved. Marna had met Dan though a friend and they had gone out once or twice. Marna was very nervous about the illegal activities but was persuaded not to report them. She had gotten expensive gifts. Marna's relationship with the stockbroker abruptly ended when he broke it off. Marna still believed that his opening up to her may have been ill advised and that he thought better of continuing to see her. As time passed, the threatening phone call seemed less important. He decided not to tell Marna.

Don called Kathy to firm up their plans to visit Gettysburg, Pennsylvania where Lincoln visited in 1863 and made his famous address. There was an excellent chance a good Lincoln memorabilia piece could be found at one of the shops. Items of interest were sometimes for sale, ordinary things, like a monogrammed hand-kerchief the president used to wipe his brow on a hot day. The two had decided to meet there since the trip would be about the same distance for both.

CHAPTER FIVE

Gettysburg was a small town with three main roads going through it. The memorial cemetery where Lincoln spoke in tribute to the Civil War battle's dead was on the outskirts. It was a sunny, brisk day. The trees were bare now and they outlined the clear blue sky as long, multi-jointed fingers in multiple directions reaching for the clouds. Don and Kathy looked in shops along Baltimore Street. The two were dressed casually in jeans and jackets. Don's was brown leather. Kathy, although older, was still pretty and her shoulder length blond hair was pulled back and fastened with an inlaid leather stay. Her lively blue eyes rested on Don as they entered the shops. The article they were looking for had been sold. However, the two of them greatly enjoyed each other's company as they looked. Kathy noticed a tintype picture of the town at the time of Lincoln's address. Don thought it was great for that period of Lincoln's life even though Lincoln is not pictured in the photograph.

The cemetery was the site of many Civil War's dead. As he walked past the spot, Don could picture Lincoln, exhausted but eloquent reciting the short but powerful speech resolving to continue the Civil War and reunite the nation.

Don and Kathy had dinner at the Dobbin House Tavern, a local bar/ restaurant. They sat down at a butcher block wooden table in a booth. There was a small crowd of people scattered about the other booths conversing jovially.

"Donny, how is everything going in New York," Kathy inquired.

"I met this wonderful woman." Don gleamed as he spoke.

"She is the best thing that has happened to me in a long time."

"Great! Tell me about her."

"Her name is Marna. We met at a party in Greenwich Village." Don shared his experience of their time together over the last three months.

"Donny, I'm glad you are happy." Kathy smiled and looked pleased.

"Listen I have something interesting to show you."

She took a book that she had brought from her car out of her purse.

"This is really creepy," she said smiling. The book, entitled The Ghosts Of Maryland, described various historic places which were haunted, several of which were of the Civil War period.

Don paged through the book with interest. "This looks pretty neat."

He put the book away, more interested in talking to his sister. He could read it later.

"How is everything going with you?" Don inquired.

Kathy was doing well as a real estate agent. She had recently gotten her real estate license. Her marriage of ten years to Bob was loving and stable.

Kathy and Don spent the night at a local motel. The next day they had breakfast at the coffee shop, hugged, said goodbye, and drove back to their respective homes.

CHAPTER SIX

The afternoon Don returned to New York he was anxious to call Marna to tell her about the trip. Marna answered the phone.

"Hello."

"Hi Marna."

"Donny I'm glad it's you."…I'm scared.

Marna had panic in her voice. Don had never heard her this way.

"What's the matter?"

"I got a threatening phone call yesterday"…they said they were going shut me up." Marna began to sob.

"Marna please don't worry," Don implored.

It was becoming clear to Don that the same people who were trying to scare him off were now threatening her.

"Marna did you recognize the person?"

"The voice sounded familiar, maybe it was John, but I'm not sure."

"Do you mean, that guy you used to date?"

"I....I don't know."

"Don't worry; I'll be right over... we can talk about it then. Don't let anybody in."

Don hurriedly left his apartment and took the elevator. He was intent on calming Marna down and if necessary, getting the police involved. He hailed a cab outside his apartment and headed for Marna's. Don's stomach tensed as the cab approached the apartment. Was Marna alright?

He quickly got out and walked briskly toward the entry door. He took the elevator to the tenth floor. As he got off, someone leaving in a hurry crashed into him, knocking him off balance and against the wall. Pain seared though his shoulder as he struggled to regain his equilibrium. Don heard rapid footsteps. He gathered himself and looked down the hall toward the elevator. The doors were closing and they were gone.

Don hurried down the hall to Marna's apartment. The door was ajar. Looking in, Don could see that the furniture was turned over and lamps were knocked off their tables, indicating a struggle had occurred. Don went over to her and felt Marna's pulse. There wasn't any. He picked up the phone and called for an ambulance. He moved her to the floor and tried to give her CPR, breathing into her mouth and giving chest compressions. *Please God, bring her back.* Although she was probably gone, Don couldn't think of anything else to do.

The paramedics arrived a few minutes later and took over. They tried to revive her, but no response. Don just stared at her lifeless body and could not believe this could happen so fast and he could do nothing to prevent it. Don's stomach turned as he struggled to comprehend the reality.

The police crowded the apartment and began to secure the crime scene. Don was told to stand outside in the hall. A middle-aged police detective dressed in a gray suit and overcoat approached him in the hallway.

"Did you know the victim?" he asked.

"Yes, we were dating," Don muttered. "Her name is Marna Anderson."

"What is your name?" The detective inquired.

"Don Kendall."

"Mr. Kendall, my name is Detective Tom Sanderson, Homicide." He handed Don a business card. Don stuffed it in his jacket pocket.

The detective was in his forties, not especially tall with thinning hair. His face was deeply lined and looked as if he had seen too much pain in life. A year ago his partner had been cut down by a shot gun in a convenience store hold-up.

"I am told that you found the victim."

"Yes."

"Do you know why anyone would want to kill Ms. Anderson?"

"I have some suspicions," Don said angrily.

"I'm sorry but I'm really not emotionally able to deal with this right now." Don looked shaken. He appeared weary and not himself.

"I see you have been though quite an ordeal."

The detective sensed Don's despair.

"Did you see anything that could help us?"

"I saw a man in the hall leaving Marna's apartment."

"Did you recognize him?"

"No, he knocked me down before I could get a look at him."

"I need for you to come down to the precinct and give us a statement."

"Okay, when?"

"Around ten tomorrow," Sanderson suggested.

"Okay," Don reluctantly agreed.

The coroner's wagon pulled up the street and parked in front of the apartment. Don waited for it seemed like hours until they brought Marna out on a stretcher, her light brown hair sticking out slightly from under the white sheet covering her face. Stunned, Don watched the vehicle as it pulled away down the street.

Don took a cab back to his apartment. There was a chilly breeze as he approached the entrance of the building. Once inside the apartment door, he took off his jacket and slumped down on the couch. *Marna is dead.* He couldn't believe it. He loved her so much. Tears welled up in his eyes and streamed down his face as he covered his eyes with the crook of his arm.

Memories of the many wonderful moments with Marna passed though his mind. He couldn't shake from his mind the picture of her lying on the couch, lifeless, gone.

He poured himself a scotch and water and gulped down the brown liquid, tasting its bitterness. Another two drinks and a haze came over him. He fell asleep.

The next day, Don woke up on the couch. It was Monday morning. He was too exhausted to go to work. The sky was overcast. He dragged himself out of bed and made some coffee. As sitting at the kitchen table sipping the vitalizing brew, he decided that he needed to go to the police station and file his report.

CHAPTER SEVEN

The precinct was in East Midtown Manhattan, on Forty-Second Street, not far from his apartment. The building was a grayish color constructed with large cinder block as many municipal buildings are. A sign on the glass above announced **New York Police Department.** He studied the business card as he walked through the double doored entrance. He found the fifth floor where the detective's office was located, walked down the hall, hesitated at a door with smoked glass in the center marked **508.** He entered the office. Detective Sanderson walked over and greeted Don. He was a serious type. Sanderson extended his hand and shook Don's.

"Hello Mr. Kendall, it is good you decided to come down today. I know that this must be difficult."

"Well, I thought it would be best to get this out of the way."

The detective escorted him though a main room of desks and into his individual office. Don followed.

"I asked you to come down here to discuss the case. There is more to the case than I let on at the apartment."

"Oh really," Don said with a look of surprise.

"Yes Mr. Kendall, Miss Anderson was involved in activities which may have led to her death."

The detective sat on his desk and faced Don sitting in a chair against the wall. The office was small, cluttered, painted in a dull green color which reminded him of and episode of Barney Miller.

"Mr. Kendall, Miss Anderson was knowledgeable of a large scale insider trading operation which was wide spread on Wall Street. We have been working with the Securities and Exchange Commission to gain enough evidence to bring about some convictions. We were working on the case for over a year. Apparently she was identified as an informant and possibly murdered because of her involvement."

It all began to make sense to Don: The car following them, the threatening phone call to him, and recently, Marna's murder.

"I was also threatened with a phone call," Don explained.

"There were other suspicious things which caused some alarm, but nothing directly threatening to Marna. I also thought that she was wearing expensive clothing and jewelry, which were apparently gifts to buy her silence. She had mentioned this guy, Dan Blackman as a person who may be involved."

"Mr. Kendall, Blackman is a suspect and there are others which we are currently investigating. Have you met any of these people?"

"No, Don replied. I hadn't even met Blackman although he apparently worked on Madison Avenue."

"She mentioned a trader named John …John Weaver…something like that, who was also part of the plan."

Detective Sanderson stood up from his chair.

"Mr. Kendall, I appreciate you coming down here. If you think of anything else, anything at all, please let me know. I will keep you informed of any developments. I am truly sorry about Miss Anderson's death and please call us with any further information you may think of or further suspicious occurrences."

"Thank you Detective." Don shook his hand and left.

It was late afternoon when Don took a cab back to the Essex. The traffic was heavy as commuters were traveling to their destinations of loved ones and contentment. Don felt neither. A chance to find someone to share his life with was gone. He didn't know how he would cope, but he had to. After entering the living room, he fixed himself a scotch and just sat for an hour. He decided to call Kathy. He needed someone to share his pain with.

The phone rang at the other end.

"Hello," Kathy answered in her usual cheerful tone.

"Hi," Don said in a voice tinged with sorrow.

"Donny, are you alright?"

Tears welled up in Don's eyes.

"Kathy, Marna has been….murdered."

"Donny, how horrible!"

"I'm really down. I don't know what I'm going to do."

Don's voice broke as he spoke. He told her about that evening and his visit to the police station. Don did not disclose the details but said that the police had suspects. He did not want Kathy to be involved.

"Donny, why don't you come over for Thanksgiving next week? Mom will be here and I will give you a chance to get your mind off things."

"Sure that sounds like a good idea," Don reluctantly agreed.

"Okay, I'll see you then. I love you, bye."

"Bye Kathy." He hung up.

That night, Don tried to sleep but it would not come. Don got up from bed and looked at the clock. It was 2:00 am. Don went into the living room to the bar and poured himself a large glass of scotch. The glass clinked when he threw in two ice cubes. He was too wound up and depressed. He sat in his Lazeboy chair, sipped the drink and put on the television. A rerun of I Love Lucy was on. Don allowed himself to be distracted by the pratfalls of the characters in black and white. He needed to drift away to another place and ease the pain. He became drowsy. Marna's face in his mind, laughing and smiling, her beautiful eyes meeting his, became a dream as he drifted off to sleep.

CHAPTER EIGHT

On Thanksgiving, Don drove down to Woodbine, Maryland. After he left the city going south on I-95 the countryside rolled by. He thought about seeing his family. It had been a year since he had seen his mother. Mary Kendall had moved from Woodlawn to Salisbury, Maryland on the eastern shore. Her husband had been estranged from the family since the divorce. He thought back to his days growing up and how she had been a great strength in his life. She always encouraged him in everything he did. She was supportive when he was playing soccer or his involvement in student government and later, his fraternity in college. He took the exit to I-695 around Baltimore and headed West on Route 70. He was on the road about four hours. Off the interstate, Don drove up a two lane road passing old farm houses up on hills with their ponds below. Livestock were scattered about the landscape. Just five miles north, he came to Woodbine. The area had new housing developments constructed where rolling acres of farmland had once been. Actually, it wasn't far from where the family lived in Baltimore County.

Kathy's house was at the end of a courtyard where modest new houses stood. Don parked his new Nissan Sentra in front and walked up to the front door and rang the doorbell. Kathy opened the door and greeted Don. Their mother also greeted him. Mary was a plump woman in her early fifties. One could see the family resemblance in her blue eyes. She wore glasses which framed her short light brown, graying hair and smooth, pretty face. As they hugged, Don felt reassured and loved. Kathy's husband, Bob, smiled broadly and shook Don's hand enthusiastically. Don threw his suitcase in the spare bedroom upstairs. The turkey dinner was in the oven, stimulating his appetite as its delicious aroma drifted throughout the house.

The family sat down for dinner and a lively, animated conversation. The remaining weekend was relaxed and joyful. He talked with his mother and learned more about her life in Salisbury. He was pleased to hear she was doing well there. She had developed friendships and a job she liked at the car rental agency where she worked. At times, Don actually forgot about the ugliness of recent days. Don said goodbye and returned to New York hopeful that he would begin to feel more positive about his life.

Don returned to work. To feel more centered, he had to get back to his regular routine. He encountered Judith in the hall. She welcomed him back to work. Relaying the events of last week and the weekend, Don was emotional. Judith expressed her sympathy. She said that she had a feeling something was going on with Marna.

Don threw himself into his work and the day went quickly. Leaving the office, he took the elevator down to the lobby and exited the front doors.

CHAPTER NINE

The screaming of ambulance sirens were heard as Don lay on the cab's back seat writhing in pain. The cab driver was shaken up but not seriously hurt. The sole driver of the other car was taken in a different ambulance.

Two paramedics carefully removed Don from the cab and strapped him to a backboard and placed a neck immobilizer around his head. Emergency lights flashed red and white as he was placed on a stretcher and loaded into the back of the ambulance. As he traveled in the ambulance with a young male paramedic, Don groaned in pain and continued to move his legs. The siren whined as they sped to New York Presbyterian Hospital.

With Don on a stretcher, the paramedics burst through the entrance of the emergency room. The ER was somewhat crowded with people sitting and waiting, some impatiently and some relaxed, reading. The smell of antiseptic permeated the room. A concerned mother sat with her ill looking son. Worried parents sat with their children waiting for sick or injured loved ones. They briefly turned their attention to the rapidly moving stretcher.

Due to the seriousness of his injuries, the paramedics quickly wheeled Don into a bay for evaluation. Two nurses and a doctor approached as the paramedic reported.

"The patient was in a broadsided car accident and may have multiple internal injuries. His breathing is regular and pulse steady."

Don blacked out.

When he awoke, a nurse was standing next to his stretcher. "Mr. Kendall, how are you now? I'm afraid you passed out a few minutes ago and we had to give you smelling salts."

Don vaguely remembered the jolting smell of the pack held under his nose to bring him to. The plump, middle-aged nurse smiled and looked business-like as she took Don's arm for a pulse. She then used a blood pressure cuff, squeezing the bulb to pump it up and stuck a thermometer in his mouth. He was quite uncomfortable as the pain had not subsided.

"That was quite and accident you were in."

"Yeah," Don mumbled just beginning to grasp the reality of his surroundings.

"Looks normal... So does your pressure," the nurse said in an oddly perky tone.

Wincing, Don muttered, "My back and neck are still hurting quite a bit and I have pain in my stomach."

"The doctor will be along soon," the nurse said, as she recorded results on a clipboard and left the room.

Don lay in the stretcher with the hard collar pinching his neck. The anxiety crept over him, not knowing what damage his body had sustained. Finally, the doctor arrived.

"Hello Mr. Kendall, I'm Doctor Strobel."

The doctor was young, in his late twenties and smiled as he addressed his patient.

"Where do you hurt?"

Don responded with difficulty. "As I explained to the nurse, my back, neck and stomach really hurt."

The doctor palpated his stomach, pushing gently. He removed the collar and touched the spinal column inquiring about the degree of pain in those areas.

"Mr. Kendall we need to get some x-rays, CAT scans and do a urinalysis and blood work to see if there is any internal damage. Do you think you will be more comfortable if we give you something for pain?"

Don nodded his head.

"Okay, I'll have the nurse give you something."

The nurse brought two small paper cups. One contained two large pills and there was water in the other. Don gratefully took the cups and consumed their contents. The nurse inserted a catheter to collect urine.

The x-ray tech arrived a few minutes later and rolled the stretcher down the hall into the x-ray room. He placed a lead vest on his patient's chest. Standing behind a lead barrier with a window, he took several x-ray films at different angles of Don's neck and upper back. In another area the CAT scan studies were also completed. Afterwards, he was wheeled back into the ER bay.

Don lay on the stretcher. The curtain was pulled, enclosing his bay. Through a gap in the front he saw nurses in white uniforms moving past. The pain medication was doing its job. As he relaxed, he began to re-experience the accident.

He was leaving work and walked onto the busy street and hailed a Checker cab. The driver was Indian, wearing a white turban. Don instructed the cabbie to take him to his apartment. The cab preceded west on 86th Street and then south on Fifth Avenue. The traffic was heavy on the four lane thoroughfare, two lanes each way. As they proceeded down the street, a black Cadillac ran a red light and quickly approached the cab on the right. The cab driver swore in Farsi as he swerved to avoid the collision. As the vehicles hit their brakes, tires squealed. The large sedan's massive grille slammed into the cab. Glass shattered and flew from the oncoming Cadillac. The cab jarred with a loud thump, metal crunched on impact. The cab was pushed across the road into the other lane. Before he could brace himself, Don was violently thrown against the back driver's side door. Pain seared through his abdomen, neck and spine as he hit the interior door and handle.

Three hours later, the doctor came into the ER bay and stood by Don's side. From the stretcher, Don looked in his direction. The doctor stuck the x-rays and the CAT scans on a viewing screen and thoughtfully examined them. He studied the clipboard with the blood work and urinalysis results.

Finally he said, "It looks like you have damage to the cartilage in your neck and multiple herniated discs in your back. Luckily, any other internal injuries are minor. There appears to be some bruising of the kidneys which needs to be monitored. We will have to admit you to the hospital."

Don looked concerned and nodded in agreement.

Don was moved to a hospital room. The bed was typical of hospitals, uncomfortable but functional with an automatic switch to lower and raise the upper half. If needed, there was a cord with a button to call the nurse. Next to him was a night stand on wheels with a drawer for personal belongings. On the other side of the bed was a tray which would extend across the bed for eating. Although there was another bed for a roommate, it was not occupied. The room had a greenish-blue theme with a bulletin board directly across from the bed with hospital announcements and policies pinned to it.

Since being admitted, he was assigned to a duty nurse on his floor. She was nice but was mostly absent due to an emergency down the hall. Before going off duty, pain medication was added to his I.V. to bring relief. Unable to sleep, Don lay in his bed, listening to a woman down the hall moaning in pain.

The morning came and the next shift came on. The nurse cheerfully said good morning and introduced herself as Sarah. She was more available and Don was pleased about the attention he was receiving.

During Don's hospitalization, Judith came to visit as well as Paulette from the office. Of course, Kathy visited and they talked about their visit to Gettysburg. Don's mother also visited and doted on him, making sure he was getting the best of care.

After three weeks, Don was ready to be discharged. The bruising to his kidneys had healed and his other injuries were stabilized. The attending physician for that floor came in and introduced herself. Don guessed that she was in her forties. She appeared experienced and competent.

"Hello Mr. Kendall, she said cheerfully. I'm doctor Powers. We are ready to send you home. I'm going to give you prescriptions for a muscle relaxer and Demerol to help with pain."

The doctor scribbled on her pad, tore them off and handed them to Don.

"You'll need a soft neck brace for at least three months. Wear it except when showering. You will also need bed rest for a few months before returning to work to speed the healing process. After you begin to get around, physical therapy will also be necessary. Check in with our outpatient department to schedule an appointment.

"Mr. Kendall you are pretty banged up, but you are lucky you are still alive. Take care of yourself." The doctor smiled at Don reassuredly and left the room.

The nurse brought a soft neck brace and put it on her patient. The pain from the injuries he sustained was extreme but it did not surpass the pain he felt from losing Marna. He would have to go on.

CHAPTER TEN

As the months progressed, winter set in. Christmas arrived and passed with no real joy. Don lay flat on his back during the required recovery period. He lay in bed and was unable to move to any degree without experiencing pain. He took the Demerol religiously. Without it, the pain was hard to bear. The sharp pain sometimes would shoot down his legs. He suffered from intermittent headaches and had difficulty sleeping. Off from work and idle, Don had a great deal of time to reflect and think. He went though each day with a lack of enthusiasm.

Kathy and Don's mother came up to New York on weekends to help Don recover. They would go to refill his prescriptions, shave and wash him up in bed. At times he propped up his head with a pillow to read or watched television but could not sustain it for long. Judith came over two to three times a week to help with meals and provide good conversation. The bedroom had high ceilings with ornate plaster trim. He studied the square designs of the tin art deco ceiling and its intricate patterns. Sunlight streamed into the room during the cold winter days.

As the months passed, the weather warmed. The trees in Central Park bloomed and leaves sprang from their branches. Regardless of the light in the room or the weather outside, Don was depressed. His condition demoralized him and he continued to dwell on Marna's death. Due to his injuries he had missed her funeral. He pictured her beautiful, lifeless body in her apartment, her future choked out of her. He wanted to forget the pain of losing her, but couldn't. He ran the events over and over in his mind.

As time passed, his thoughts also dwelled on Abraham Lincoln's life and the tragic events of his death. He pictured his body lying in a sideway position as his long legs would not fit on the bed as he lay mortally wounded.

He thought about the conspiracy to kill Lincoln and he pictured Mary Saratt and the three co-conspirators: Lewis Powell, George Atzerolt, Lewis Paine and David Herold. The others were a ragtag bunch, but Mary's more noble visage kept re-occurring in his mind. Was she guilty? Regardless, she had been hanged for her role in the plot.

After a time, Don drifted off to sleep. He pictured Mary's handsome forty-two year old face smiling at him. She was plain, without any makeup but pretty, her brown hair tied back in a bun off her face. In his dream, the visage spoke to him "Donald I know the truth." When he awoke later that day, Don thought about making a connection with her somehow.

Over time, Don was able to use a wheelchair. He asked Judith to bring him books about spiritualism and the occult. He read several of them as well as the book Kathy had given him: The Ghosts of Maryland. Could there be another dimension or another "side" that people pass to after they die?

Don was becoming more and more motivated to begin writing his book. With his vast knowledge of Lincoln's life and death, he was the person that could bring forth new ideas.

CHAPTER ELEVEN

New York Presbyterian Hospital in Washington Heights was a modern, sleek building with arched entrances and tinted glass windows. The day was warm and pleasant. Don was glad to be around again and not confined to his apartment. He was walking now. Although somewhat apprehensive about taking a cab, he had no choice but to utilize one.

Don gingerly walked in the front entrance, checked the directory on the wall in the lobby to remind him of the location of the outpatient clinic for his doctor's appointment. He walked down the hall through an entrance way. The receptionist greeted him as he walked up to the counter.

"Hello, I'm Don Kendall... I have an appointment with Dr. Abramson."

"Hello Mr. Kendall. The doctor will be right with you."

Don found a seat in the waiting area. There was modern furniture typical of that type of office: couches, comfortable chairs and end tables cluttered with magazines. He had previously been there after the accident for his a follow-up after leaving the hospital. Don began to think back to the total lack of mobility he sustained from the injuries the months he spent in bed healing. He had come a long way since then and wondered if he would ever be normal again.

"The doctor will see you now," the receptionist reported.

Don went though the door, down a small hall to an examination room. He entered and sat on the examination table covered with thin paper. A few minutes later Dr. Abramson lightly knocked on the closed door and entered.

"Hello Mr. Kendall," the doctor said cheerfully.

He was in his early forties with slightly graying temples. He wore round wire rimmed glasses perched on his pointed nose which centered his long face. He looked down them as he gazed at Don.

"How are you feeling today?"

"Well doctor, I am getting around. My neck is somewhat better but the pain in my back is still intense at times."

"Are you still taking the Demerol prescribed in the ER?"

"Doctor, the Demerol is not working. I don't think the dose is strong enough."

"What kind of pain is it?"

"It's a throbbing pain in my mid and lower back. Sometimes it travels down my legs."

The doctor paged through the medical record he obtained from the hospital while he spoke.

"Did you go to the physical therapist I recommended?"

"Yes, I have had twelve weeks of sessions. I went three times a week."

"Did it help?" The doctor inquired.

"Yes, but only some."

"Due to the severity of your injury I am going to increase the Demerol from fifty to one hundred milligrams. Let me know if this makes you more comfortable. Schedule another appointment in three weeks with the receptionist."

"Thank you doctor," Don said gratefully.

A few weeks later, when Don returned to work it was a chore to him. He had trouble getting out of bed in the morning. He missed Marna desperately. His back pain prevented him from standing for any length of time when making presentations. When sitting he was still uncomfortable. The physical therapy had improved his neck considerably and he had little trouble with it. However, his back had its range of motion but he would have the pain for the rest of his life.

After arriving at work Don decided to call Detective Sanderson. He took out the business card the detective had given him and dialed the number. Sanderson picked up the phone himself. Don, expecting a secretary to answer was somewhat surprised.

"Hello.... Detective Sanderson?"

"This is Don Kendall."

"Hello Mr. Kendall. What can I do for you?"

"Do you remember the murder of my girlfriend Marna Anderson?"

"Of course. It was about seven months ago in Chelsea."

"Have you made any progress in the case?" Don was a little perturbed the detective wasn't forthcoming with any further information.

"I'm afraid we have not been able to establish any concrete leads on it. The individuals you mentioned checked out in our initial investigation. Mr. Weaver was out of town the day of the murder and we have not been able to find Blackman."

"You mean he has disappeared?"

"I'm afraid so."

"What about the Wall Street investigation?"

"Since Ms. Anderson was our main witness, we could not gather enough evidence to turn the case over to the Securities and Exchange Commission for charges."

"Do you mean Marna died for nothing?" Don said angrily.

"I'm sorry Mr. Kendall. We pursued it as recently as a month ago and had to put our priorities elsewhere. I did not hear from you with any further information so I assumed that you could not think of anything else. I had no need to bother you with any other questions." Don was disappointed and angered.

"Well detective, I guess we don't have much else to talk about."

"I'm sorry Mr. Kendall. I had hoped for more."

"Bye detective."

Don hung up the phone and sat in stunned silence, thinking.

Later that day, Don saw Judith in the hall and asked her to have lunch. They went to a small restaurant on Madison Avenue. They sat at a table by a window of the busy place and watched the passers by. They were dressed in summer shorts and tops. The sun shone brightly. It was obvious that Don had something on his mind. He broached the subject after they ordered.

"Judith I'm having trouble staying focused at work."

"I have noticed," Judith said concerned.

"Is it your back?"

"Yes, it still hurts at times although I am on Demerol. I'm trying to follow the prescription and not take any more."

He lied. In fact the dosage of one hundred milligrams he recently got was not holding him. He had to take them more often and his prescription refill was running out. Don looked in the distance and reflected on his thoughts while taking a bite of his sandwich.

"Marna was so important in my life…I don't know what I am going to do without her."

"I know," Judith said empathically.

"You have to move past this…I know you can… you are such a strong, resourceful person."

"I need to have closure. I'm going to try and find Dan Blackman. The police are out of leads. I talked to the detective today. Maybe through my contacts on Madison Avenue I can track him down. He is the only link I have to Marna's murder.

"Do you think that is wise?" Judith said concerned.

"I need to know why she died and who killed her. I will inform the police of anything I find."

"Don, I hope you are not going to become obsessed by this."

"No. Absolutely not. In fact, I have decided to go to Springfield to research a book about Lincoln."

"Don, I think that is a great idea." Judith was quite aware of Don's interest in Lincoln. Don did not reveal his vivid dream about Mary Saratt.

"Don, I'm worried about you."

"I know things have been rough. I will be alright," Don said, looking unconvinced.

"You know that if you need anything from me you can count on it." Judith smiled with sincerity.

After work Don returned to his apartment. He put down his brief case exhausted and immediately poured himself a large scotch from the bar. He gulped it down and took two of the white tablets. Don dropped down on the couch adjacent to the bar. He waited for the spreading haze to wash over him. It did as he expected. He went to a place of no pain or grief. Where everything was numb and bliss.

The next morning Don woke up in his bed. He didn't remember how he got there. He pulled himself together and went in to the office.

He paged though his Rolodex to think of anyone who could have known Blackman. Marna had mentioned a firm in passing but Don could place it now. He called a friend who started in the business eight years ago as he had. He punched in the numbers and reached a secretary who put him through.

"Hi Wade, this is Don Kendall."

Wade was pleasantly surprised to hear from him.

"Don, how are you? I heard that you were in a car accident."

"I'm doing well, Don lied. I'm back on my feet after seven months."

"Don, that's great. I'm glad that you are back to work."

"Thanks."

Don decided to get to the point.

"I am calling to track down a guy who worked on Madison Avenue about a year ago. Did you know a guy named Dan Blackman?"

"Yeah, I think he was an exec at Armani. Are you looking to set up a deal?"

"No, this is a personal matter."

"Thanks Wade, It's been good talking to you. We'll have lunch sometime."

"You're welcome Don."

"Anytime."

"Don hung up and quickly looked in his Rolodex for the Armani office number."

The receptionist answered in a pleasant tone. "Armani Corporation."

"Is there a Dan Blackman at that office?"

"Yes sir, I will ring his extension."

Don couldn't believe it was this easy. Surely the police must have checked this out. The phone rang four times and the answering machine picked up.

"This is Dan Blackman; I'm not in the office right now, so please leave me a message." He decided not to leave a message, hung up and redialed the number. He asked the receptionist to put him through to the director of marketing.

"Hello, this is Bill Murphy."

"Hello Bill this is Don Kendall at Klein and Associates. I am trying to reach Dan Blackman."

Don was beginning to become tense. He didn't want to be identified but had no choice.

"Well, Dan has been on extended leave. What is this about?"

"I was following up on a conversation we had about some marketing ideas."

"Okay, I'll let him know you called. Give me your number." Don did not want to give any further information. He had already taken too much of a chance. These people were dangerous.

"Thanks, I'll get back to him another time."

Don hung up. He had located Blackman who apparently still had a job at Armani. This was something. The police must have learned the same thing but still had not found him for questioning. Don assumed that considering the extensive crime rate, white collar crime was not much of a priority in New York City. There were so many murders, Marna's had gotten lost in the shuffle. Don had to take his pain medication. His back was throbbing.

A few weeks passed and Don had not made any progress in finding Blackman.

Finally, Don tracked down Blackman's apartment address through mutual associates he had worked with in the advertising business. It was a luxury apartment in SoHo. After visiting the place and talking to the landlord he had found that Blackman had moved out. It figured.

CHAPTER TWELVE

The National Archives in Washington D.C. stood between Pennsylvania and Constitution Avenues. The massive building, occupying two city blocks, preserved most of the important documents in American history which included the Declaration of Independence, the Bill Of Rights and the Constitution. Wanting to find information to support his theory, Don traveled there from New York.

Don drove his car up the ramp of the parking garage on First Street and found a space on the level marked **Six**. He took the elevator down to the ground level and walked out onto First Street. After acclimating himself, he began walking down First Street in the direction of Constitution Avenue. I was a warm, late-summer day. He walked past Capitol Hill on his left. After traveling several blocks, the Capital Building appeared right in front of him. Its large dome rose to the clear blue sky with the Statue of Freedom perched on top of her wreathed pedestal. She was draped in a flowing garment, feathered helmet on her head holding a wreath in one hand

and a sheathed sword to her side in the other—seeming to gaze over the entire city. As he approached Constitution Avenue, Don noticed the gleaming white granite steps of the Capital Building front entrance. Tourists were scattered on the front sidewalk and on the steps moving toward the entrance. He continued to walk.

When approaching Constitution, he made a right and headed the four blocks toward the archives building. Cars were parked along the busy, six lane street and traffic light poles sat on the corners of the intersections with twin street lights on top. Don noticed, but not for the first time, that there were no directional lights hanging in the middle of the street as in other cities. He remembered driving though the city passing a red light that wasn't there and being confused by its traffic circles.

Don passed the U.S. Court House and then the Federal Trade Commission Building on his side of the street and the National Gallery of Art across the thoroughfare. He approached the entrance to the archives. Looking like a Roman palace, the wide majestic white steps led to tall Corinthian columns, eight across, supporting a triangular façade of human figures—some appearing as guardians of knowledge, others looking as if in a struggle with each other—under which **Archives Of The United State Of America** was engraved. Green trees on each side stood out superimposed by the white granite building behind them. Substantial iron light stanchions, green from weathering with five white glass globes adorned each side of the building.

As Don entered the building, he passed other Corinthian columns, three deep. Huge bronze doors stood open before him as he walked into the impressive main hall. Paintings of the founding fathers standing together in historic scenes were mounted on each side of the room. In the middle, the Declaration of Independence was displayed in a thick, hermetically sealed, bulletproof glass case. Other permanent document displays were at the front of the glossy, gray and white marble floor inlaid with squares of darker gray marble with a matching circle in each.

An information desk was on the right near the wall. Don approached it to inquire about the location of the documents he sought. He checked his watch. It was 12:30, with time to spare before the 1:30 pull time. A stern looking rent-a-cop sat at a desk in a dark blue uniform. He looked at Don, his glazed over, brown eyes peered below the bill of his uniform hat.

"I'm looking for financial documents related to the Whitehouse," Don said.

"You have to go to the research room to register," the guard informed him.

The guard pointed to his right as he spoke.

"Take the elevator to the left, down to the first level and check in there."

Don took the elevator down to the room. It was set up like a visitor's center—chairs were lined up in the middle. There were tables lining the walls with chairs around them. Facing the front was a long desk, with two federal employees behind it.

An employee, dressed in a sport coat and tie, his photo I.D. clipped to his lapel, addressed him as he approached.

"Are you here to register?" he said in an official tone.

"Yes," Don said smiling.

"May I see a form of identification?"

"Will a driver's license suffice?" Don said reaching for his wallet.

The young man took it, inspected the photograph, looked at Don and back. He handed it back to him.

"Have you ever been to the National Archives before?"

"Yes, a couple of years ago."

"So you know our regulations about using your own pens, pencils or paper. We will supply them to you if you ask. There are no cameras, or briefcases allowed. Copies are ten cents in the copy room."

"Please fill this form out, and come back."

Don took the one page form to a table at the side of the room and after completing it, returned it to the clerk.

The young man studied the form, digesting the information. Looking up, he addressed his visitor. "All the archived Whitehouse records are downstairs on the second lower level. You will have to check the card catalogs and pull a research card, give it to the clerk and show your I.D."

Don arrived at the lower floor and walked off the elevator. The lined up cabinets of card files in drawers covered the expanse of the room. Florescent lights in the ceiling shone brightly. He felt overwhelmed at first but by process of elimination, he found the period—1853 to 1870.

Don took the elevator down to the next floor. When the doors opened, in front of him was a door marked **Executive Branch Documents** above it. He walked into the room. It was a modern looking place unlike the stuffy library he had imagined. Throughout the room there were two-person desks adjoining each other with an eighteen-inch glass pane separating the seats. People with white gloves on sat at their places studying bound volumes or pages in front of them. At the front of the room was a perky looking young woman, a brunette with long hair and red framed glasses, perhaps in her mid-twenties, seated at a desk in front facing the examination desks. She sat attentively watching the people at the desks in the room. Don imagined that it must be quite a responsibility to care for such valuable documents. To the right of her there was a raised tier of rooms with numbers on the doors where the documents were stored. An exposed spiral staircase with a thin rail led up to the document rooms.

Don walked up to the young woman sitting at the desk.

"I am interested in looking at these bound volumes."

"Microfiche or paper?"

"I'll start with paper."

He handed her the research card with the numbers on it. She looked at it and then shifted her gaze to Don.

"May I see a form of identification?"

"Sure." Don took out his driver's license and held it up for her. She seemed satisfied.

"Please use these gloves when you handle the documents."

Don put the gloves on.

"Wait here."

The woman got out of her chair with the card in her hand and ascended the stairs. After ten minutes, the woman returned with a box of bound volumes. She placed the box on the desk.

"Sign here." Don scribbled his name on the page.

She handed him a box which contained ten ledgers from The Department of The Interior Disbursing Office. He took them over, and put them down on the desk, and sat down. He picked up a ledger and began looking through it. He continued to study the others until at last, he found the important documents he was looking for.

After his return to New York from Washington, Don began making plans for a trip to Springfield Illinois. Abraham Lincoln lived there from 1837 to 1861, leaving when he was elected president. He first went there to take a job as junior law partner. He established a home, married and had a family in Springfield. The Lincoln Presidential Library was a great source of information and the Lincoln House was a national historic site. Don had been there three years ago with Kathy and had found it of great interest. This time he wanted to go with a different purpose in mind. His visit to the National Archives had been productive but he needed more documentation.

He made reservations at a hotel one mile from Lincoln's home and the library. He decided to drive. An airplane would be too confining. He never liked flying anyway. He felt that he could take his time, enjoy the scenery, and make stops where he wished. If his back pain were too much, he would be able to get out of the car and stretch. Don called Kathy to find out if she wanted to go. She was wrapped up with several real estate deals and could not get away.

CHAPTER THIRTEEN

Don set out in early fall for Springfield. He drove his light green Nissan over I-80 across Pennsylvania. The weather was pleasant and the sun shone brightly as he drove. He was glad to get out of the office and do something different. It had been a year since he had met Marna and he was thinking about her. His sadness had faded giving way to fond memories. He put in his newly bought cassette tape of the Eagles. The guitar introduction to *Hotel California* began to play and Don Henley began to sing about a dark desert highway.

Don greatly enjoyed the music as he drove. He traveled for several hours through Pennsylvania and crossed the Ohio line when he noticed a dark blue, full sized sedan following him. Most of the other cars on the road were smaller mid-sized or compacts. As he drove, the traffic picked up, and other vehicles filled the lanes around him and he didn't see the dark blue sedan. Don thought to himself *you really must be getting paranoid. That couldn't be the car following us in New York before Marna was murdered.*

As he drove for another hour, the traffic thinned, revealing the dark blue car which was still there. Don studied it in his rear view mirror. It was a Crown Victoria, similar to the car outside the Peacock Restaurant. Don became apprehensive but kept driving. *It can't really be the car.* The sedan started to speed up and moved in directly behind him. Don tried to remain relaxed and increased his speed and moved to the inside of the two lanes. As the highway became more isolated with just countryside and an occasional house, the Crown Vic moved up beside Don's Sentra. Don looked over and saw the driver wearing sunglasses and one passenger next to him. The Crown Vic veered towards Don's Sentra, trying to force him off the road. In an effort to avoid a collision, Don braked slightly and swerved to the left. It was no use. The Crown Vic was on him. It smashed into Don's Sentra, sideswiping it. Don felt the impact of the blow and heard metal crunch. He didn't have time to think and just reacted instinctively. He slammed on the brakes. His tires screeched and the Sentra abruptly slowed and let the Crown Vic go by. Don quickly took an exit in front of him. Don had no idea where he was, but continued on and followed the local road off the exit. It was more rural with woods on either side. He nervously checked his rear view mirror for the Crown Vic. It wasn't there. Don kept driving trying to get some distance between him and his pursuers. He drove down the two lane road just following it, to see how he could get back to the main highway. He drove for about two miles when the Crown Vic appeared directly behind him. It must have come in from a side road on the left. The large grill of the Crown Vic rammed the back of the Sentra. The Sentra bolted. Don accelerated and tried to outrun the aggressive vehicle on the hilly road. At eighty miles-per-hour he hit a rise and went airborne. The Sentra violently landed, hit the asphalt, its shocks banging, sparks flying. The Crown Vic followed and hit the rise, landed and skidded off the side of the road into a ditch. Dirt flew onto its windshield as it plowed into the side of a hill. Don continued to drive down the road. He quickly checked his side mirror and saw that the dark blue car was stuck in the embankment.

Don slowed but kept a speed higher than necessary. He began to calm down. His adrenaline began to slow and his breathing returned to normal. While checking his rearview mirror for any sign of the Crown Vic, he wandered down several roads, eventually finding signs indicating a route West to Columbus, Ohio.

Don turned on the tape deck again. The hard rock sounding guitar intro to *Life in the Fast Lane* began to play. *How appropriate,* he thought.

Don drove into Columbus and decided to spend the night there. His back was hurting and he was tired. He decided to check in at a local motel. Nervously getting out of the car, he looked around and saw no evidence of his pursuers. He looked at his new car. The driver's side was scraped from the rear of the driver's door to the front fender which was bent forward. The rear fender was completely smashed in but miraculously had stayed on. Don was sick to see the damage to his new car but felt lucky to be alive. Besides, he had car insurance.

Once in his room, Don put his suit case on the luggage rack. He opened the suitcase and took out his pain medication and gulped down three of them. His back had taken a beating. He was in excruciating pain. He took a bottle of Red and Black scotch out of the bag, poured himself a full glass from the motel, and drank it without bothering to get any ice. His nerves began to calm down and the pain began to numb as he sipped the drink in the arm chair next to the bed. He picked up the phone to call the police but what was the point? The incident has happened hours ago back off of I-80 somewhere and they were probably long gone by now.

Don drifted off to sleep in the chair. He jerked awake as the neon sign flashing **Buckeye Motel** outside splashed light in his face. He got up, changed into his pajamas and lay on the bed. He thought about his harrowing experience of the dark blue Crown Victoria pursuing him. *Who was it?* The threatening voice on the phone at his apartment a year ago echoed in his head; *something might happen to you.*

They really must want me dead.

CHAPTER FOURTEEN

Don arrived into Springfield two days later. He checked into the Hilton Springfield Hotel which he had reserved two weeks earlier. He decided to have breakfast and make plans for the day. He wanted to go to the Lincoln Library and if he had time, visit Lincoln's home.

The restaurant was small but adequate for thirty people. It was ironically called the Manhattan Grille Room reminiscent of downtown New York. It really did look like an intimate restaurant with plush chairs and small tables adorned with flower arrangements in the center of them. There was a tapestry on the wall and busy, ornate carpeting. Don thought ironically, *I come to Illinois and I'm back in New York.* The glasses clinked in the background and a smattering of people talking filled the room. He looked around nervously for anyone paying close attention to him as if he could actually identify his pursuers.

After breakfast, Don drove his dented Nissan to the library. It wasn't far—one mile. He pulled into the parking lot of the library.

The front entrance of the building, dating back to 1889, had five tall multi-paned windows making up a circular structure with skylights at the top. This set off a municipal type building made of large tan block.

Don went inside and asked for the clerk to inform him of his appointment. After confirming his research needs with the clerk, he looked in the card catalog for references about Mary Saratt and Mary Todd. He pulled a number of bound memoirs and letters from the stacks and spent several hours taking notes. Now satisfied that he had gotten most of what he wanted, he returned to the hotel.

As he drove back to the hotel, the sun was beginning to set. He hadn't realized he had been at the library so long. After taking the elevator up to his room on the fifth floor he put his key in the door and heard someone inside. Don quickly entered the room and found a short man with a muscular build bent over, looking through his belongings.

Don yelled, "What the hell are you doing!"

As the intruder tried to get to the door, Don lunged toward him blocking his path. Don could feel the anger building within him—his face was red, his fists balled up.

"I'm tired of this shit!" Don shoved the man hard. He stumbled backward, hitting the wall. Intent on getting out of the room, he got up, bulled ahead— forcefully pushed Don, and lunged for the door, flinging it open. He scampered out into the hallway. Don recovered and ran outside. The exit door at the end of the hall was still closing. The intruder must have gone through it. Don ran down the hall and bolted though the door. He glimpsed the man and heard the intruder's footsteps descending the concrete steps of the fire exit. Don went though the door but the man was too fast. He would never catch him. Frustrated, Don stopped, gasping for air. His back was beginning to throb from the exertion.

When Don returned to the room, he sat on the bed and surveyed the scene. The room had been tossed. The end tables had been searched, the drawers left on the floor. His belongings were removed from his suitcase and were strewn all over the floor along with the contents of the closet.

Don thought about the intruder's appearance. Did he look like the man driving the Crown Vic? He struggled to get a picture in his mind but he wasn't sure. At least he had seen this guy close up.

The next day, Don's theory continued to formulate in his mind as he visited the Lincoln's home. Although he was still thinking about the intruder at his hotel, he pressed on with his plans for the trip.

The historical site was preserved in great detail and looked much like it did when the family lived there before moving to Washington D.C.

It was a two story dwelling with white clapboard siding and eight windows with green shutters in the front—five on top and four on the bottom. The sides of the house which extended to the back of the property also had several windows. A white fence with stanchions on the corners and two lengths of horizontal fencing boards surrounded the house. He walked up the steps in the front through a wide doorway. A woman dressed in a brown National Park Service uniform asked him about a tour. He declined. Don walked though the house which was decorated with period furniture and wall hangings. A book case and desk stood next to a window in the library. On the bookshelf were displayed tattered volumes of books Lincoln had left behind when moving. He went into the parlor. A portrait of Mary was hanging on the wall.

By the end of his visit to Springfield, it became clear to him that the premise for his book would focus on Mary Todd Lincoln.

CHAPTER FIFTEEN

A week later, Don returned to New York. He called Kathy to tell her about the trip and his progress on the premise for his book. Don decided not to tell her about the strange events during the trip. He couldn't really prove anything and was afraid that he was beginning to sound paranoid. Besides, he didn't want to burden her with his problems. He had to solve this himself. Kathy was glad to hear from him and was enthusiastic to hear about the trip.

That night after returning to his apartment, he could not sleep. He had taken a dose of Demerol as usual, but he tossed and turned. He pictured Marna's lifeless body, her face blue, hair and limbs in different directions. He thought about the Crown Vic on the road behind him closing in. Frightening images of struggling with the Sentra steering wheel, losing control, overturning, tumbling over and over and smashing into a hundred pieces formed in his imagination.

Thinking back to the encounter at the hotel, Don vainly tried to picture the face of the mysterious man bolting from his room.

He decided that it was no use, got up, took another two tablets and sat in the Lazeboy chair trying to clear the horrible images. The sedative effect of the additional Demerol did not kick in. He sat up for hours thinking. The sunlight of dawn entered the room forming shadows of the blinds on the wall. It was morning. He decided that he had to return to the clinic to get something for sleep.

Don returned to work but was preoccupied with identifying his pursuer. He had to find Dan Blackman who seemed to be the key to everything. He ran into Judith and filled her in on the places he had visited and that he was making progress on his book. He reiterated his desire to find Blackman and that the trip had not changed his mind.

A few weeks later, Don got a break. He got a call from Bill Murphy, the contact at Armani he had talked to. His secretary, Paulette put the call through. He hadn't left a forwarding number but his company was listed.

"Hi Bill."

"Hello Don. I have some information you may be interested in."

"Don, I have an address for Dan Blackman."

"Oh really, I had figured that he had left the company."

"Actually, he has but he called to give us a forwarding address in case any mail came to the office for him. I know over the years we have had a good business relationship and we want to continue that."

"I appreciate it."

Don couldn't believe his luck. A new address had fallen into is lap.

"The address is in New Jersey... Falstaff Apartments on thirteen-twenty Falstaff Lane, apartment three-ten."

"Thanks Bill, this is a big help."

The next day, Don drove though the Holland Tunnel to New Jersey to track down the address. He had not slept well for weeks and was exhausted. He used a map to find the street and eventually came to a suburban neighborhood in East Orange. After some driving around he found the modern apartment complex. It was a rainy day. The leaves from the trees on the street fell wet and stuck to the pavement.

Don parked his car. After he got out, he was reminded of his scare in Ohio by the dents still in the side and the back. He never had bothered to get them fixed.

The apartment complex was laid out into courts with six one story apartments on each. Number three-hundred was up a rise at the top of a flight of steps. It rained lightly, leaving small drops on the shoulders of Don's jacket and in his hair. As he looked for the apartment, he began to get angry, not a mood he easily got into.

Don took a breath and rang the doorbell. A man, taller than Don, appearing lankier, opened the door. He had dark curly hair and a long face with a strong chin. *This doesn't look at all like the guy at the hotel.*

"Can I help you?" the man asked looking a little bothered.

"Are you Dan Blackman?"

"I might be… who are you?"

"Don Kendall, a friend of Bill Murphy at Armani."

The man dropped his guard somewhat.

"Oh yeah, Bill…I don't work there any more."

"Did you know a woman named Marna Anderson?"

"Yes, but not very well." Blackman began to look nervous. "What's this about?"

"She's dead, and I think you know who killed her."

Blackman's demeanor suddenly changed. "Listen it wasn't me! I swear."

Making an effort to control his anger, Don stepped though the doorway and moved towards him.

"What do you know about it?"

"All I know is that we were making some stock trades that were very profitable. John Weaver handled it on Wall Street. I just introduced him to Marna."

Don believed him. "Marna told me about that."

Don stepped closer to Blackman. "Did Weaver kill her?"

"I don't know! Honestly, I don't."

Don looked at Blackman locking eyes with him.

"Where is he?"

"He's in Baltimore... moved there a few months ago. He left Wall Street a millionaire."

"Baltimore...where?"

"He has an apartment in the Mount Vernon area."

Blackman was becoming agitated.

"You need to get out of here!" He said angrily.

Blackman swung at Don and hit him in the side of the face. Don reeled back, his adrenaline pumping. His face had a large red mark on the side and it stung. He ran at Blackman hard, swung and hit him with all his might. The impact jolted Blackman but did not bring him down. Before Blackman could react, Don tackled him at the waist and the two of them went toward a coffee table in the center of the room.

Blackman struck his head on the side as they fell.

Don looked beneath him at Blackman. His head was bleeding profusely on the side. He wasn't moving. A pool of blood was beginning to form under his head. The red substance was coming out fast. Don got up on his feet. He looked at his shirt which had blood all over the front. He panicked.

"Oh my god, I killed him."

The people next door heard the commotion and came to investigate. The door was still wide open. A middle aged man and a couple of teenagers were walking down the path. Don quickly scooted out the door, partially covering his face with his jacket.

Don speeded toward New York. It had stopped raining and the road was still wet. He was sweating and breathing heavily. He slowed the car as he began to calm down and collect himself. He really didn't mean to kill Blackman and began to curse himself for leaving the scene the way he did. Now he would look guilty. As he drove back to his apartment, he began to think that the best thing to do was to call the police and tell them.

After arriving, he took off his coat, laid it on the sofa and picked up the phone. He still had the detective's card on the table and began to dial the numbers.

A voice announced, "NYPD." Don hung up. He couldn't take a chance that he would be blamed.

CHAPTER SIXTEEN

The following Monday, Don had lunch with Judith as they had in the past. Michael's Café was on Madison Avenue, a few blocks south from their building. On the way, Don picked up a *New York Times* from the news stand outside the door. He was early. Judith was delayed in a meeting.

The café was typical of others in New York. The aroma of food permeated the place: hamburgers and bacon frying on the grille, toasted bread popping up, coffee brewing and French fries cooking in their baskets of oil. There was an eat-in counter and small tables and booths with one of those machines with a list of records to flip through and play; three for a quarter. The place was crowded with other business types for lunch. Don had selected a booth and found a seat there.

As he paged though the *New York and Region* section and in the *Police Blotter* column, he noticed an item: **N.J. Man Assaulted; Left For Dead**

Alarmed, Don read the article.

Residents of Falstaff Apartments found an unidentified man in his residence yesterday. A neighbor, age 58 reported to police that he heard two men arguing at the apartment complex about 2:00 pm on Saturday. Witnesses observed the other man in the altercation flee the scene. The neighbor reported that he and two other residents investigated the noise and found the man on the floor of the apartment who was unresponsive. Authorities are asking anyone with information call the New Jersey State Police.

As Don's anxiety increased, he began to sweat. *This had to be Blackman.* He made an effort to collect himself. *It was an accident. I'm not really guilty of anything. Relax. The police have no idea who it is. They can't link it to me anyway.*

When Judith arrived, she sat in the booth facing the cashier next to the door. She noticed how tired Don looked. Immersed in an advertising project that she was putting together, she hadn't seen him much over the last few weeks.

"Don, how are you? You look terrible," she said concerned.

Don tried to hide the strain he had experienced over the last several weeks but it was pretty obvious.

"Well, I haven't been sleeping very well lately and I am thinking about seeing my doctor."

"Don, I think that would be a good idea."

Don decided to change the subject. "I think I have made some progress in finding Marna's murderer."

"Oh... really?" Judith's eyes widened, showing interest.

"I was able to get in touch with Dan Blackman through work contacts." Trying to disguise his guilt, Don left out the part about going to his apartment.

"He gave me information about John Weaver. He was up to his ass in this thing. He probably had a hand in her murder if he didn't do it himself. He left his job on Wall Street and lives in Baltimore now."

"It really sounds like you are making progress."

"Well, it's coming along."

"I'm planning to travel to Baltimore to find him. I haven't seen my mother for a long time and I'll probably go to Salisbury first."

Later that week, Don called the clinic at New York Presbyterian to make an appointment. The only way he could fall asleep was with large doses of Demerol with a drink or two. Even then, he woke up during the night. He would lie awake all night staring at the ceiling until morning came. His job performance suffered but Don was able to disguise it. Even Judith didn't notice. Exhausted, Don would not go to work some days.

On the day of his appointment, he entered the modern building and found the outpatient clinic. He checked in and found a seat in the waiting room.

He was soon escorted to the examination room by a nurse. He described the insomnia to Dr. Abramson leaving out the fact he was abusing his Demerol and drinking alcohol. The doctor was sympathetic but warned Don about the dangers of taking too much of a combination of sedative and pain medication.

Don convinced the doctor that he would not have any problem and would be careful. The doctor prescribed a small dose of Methaqualone for sleep.

Methaqualone was a nervous system depressant. Don's dose, one hundred-fifty milligrams was the minimum. Its function was to produce a quiet, deep, sleep by producing a depression of brain function. Don was unaware of its nickname "Ludes" and its illegal use on New York disco night clubs, such as Studio 54, to produce an alcohol like effect.

After purchasing the pills at the pharmacy, Don returned to his apartment. When he was ready for bed, he took one of the tablets. He looked at the label. There were quite a few side effects. He read that frequent use could result in anxiety, hallucinations, and delusions. He didn't care; he wanted to sleep.

CHAPTER SEVENTEEN

Don traveled south to Salisbury, Maryland. He had taken vacation time from his firm. Things were beginning to come apart. He was a nervous wreck that he would be discovered and implicated in his accidental killing of Dan Blackman. His work performance had suffered but he was able to successfully cover it up. He needed to go somewhere for a respite from the hustle and bustle of New York.

Salisbury was two hundred miles south. On the Eastern Shore of Maryland, the area was quite rural, best known in the state for the Purdue chicken industry. Many Marylanders drove through the small town on the way to Ocean City, fifty miles to the East. Mary Kendall lived in a suburban area near Salisbury State College. In the neighborhood were older, distinguished looking individual houses with small yards and gray slate roofs. Well kept flower gardens adorned the yards.

Don drove down the small residential street and parked in front of the house. Memories of his wonderful relationship with his mother flowed forth. They were very close. She had been the mainstay in his life, mostly due to the departure of his father when growing up. Don had to steel himself in order to put on a front for her. He didn't want her to know about his growing dependency on pain medication and especially his incident with Blackman. He was certain that he could skirt any questions relating to these matters.

Don rang the doorbell.

"Donny! It's great to see you," she said as he crossed the threshold holding a small suitcase.

Mary gave him a big hug and held on for a few minutes as Don hugged back. Her Irish setter, Molly, pranced into the room with her tail wagging in anticipation of being petted by the visitor. When Don entered the living room the dog rubbed against him, her wet nose probing his pant leg and he reciprocated by petting her on the head.

It had been over a year since Don and his mother had seen each other. Mary had cared for him after the auto accident when Don was bedridden. Don had always felt safe in her presence. He knew that he would be accepted and not be judged by her. He could be a mass murderer for Christ's sake and Mom would forgive him. Still, he could not tell her about his life since the crash. He didn't want her opinion of him to diminish.

Mary Kendall looked attractive for her fifty-three years. Her blue eyes showed excitement to see her son. She smiled as she led him into the small, but well decorated living room.

Don left his suitcase next to the wall. They sat on a tan love seat facing a small stone fireplace. They had coffee in mugs decorated with a pair of snow men staring blankly with coal eyes, multi-colored hats and scarves, stick arms, holding a broom in a snow drift.

"Donny how is your back?" Mary said with concern.

"I'm doing OK," Don lied.

"I am taking medication for pain which is helping a great deal. I also had physical therapy for a while and my flexibility is better. I am doing stretches each day."

Don tried to change the subject. I have talked to Kathy… she is doing great. Her real estate business is taking off. Carroll County is growing tremendously."

"I'm glad to hear that. How's your job going?" Mary inquired.

"It's going great." Don did a good job of hiding his growing impatience with Madison Avenue.

"I'm giving serious thought to writing full time. I have some great ideas about a book."

"Don't tell me… Abraham Lincoln," Mary said, kidding him.

"You guessed it."

"You aren't going to leave your job are you?" Mary said concerned. "You have worked to hard to be a success."

Don felt some guilt about his growing disenchantment at working in New York. After all, he was at the top of his profession. "Well Mom, I'm just thinking about it now… I haven't decided anything yet."

Don spent ten days at his mother's home. They wiled away their time together talking about his childhood in Woodlawn. They looked at old snapshots of the family. Don hadn't laughed so much in a long time. Later in the week they took a trip to Ocean City, where many summer vacations were spent. Since most tourists left after Labor Day, traffic was light and the beach was mostly empty. A few people, scattered over the beach, were dressed in shorts and tee shirts. The air was brisk and the sun was warm enough to enjoy the beach. Only a few people went swimming. They spent the afternoon in beach chairs enjoying the sea air. Later, they went to lunch at Phillips, a well known local seafood restaurant.

Don left Salisbury. Relaxed, he headed toward Baltimore to learn more about Marna's killer.

CHAPTER EIGHTEEN

Don drove across the Eastern shore of Maryland enroute to Baltimore. It was mostly rural: little towns, farms with silos and cattle grazing in fields. Crops of corn, string beans and melons were out of season now.

He crossed the Chesapeake Bay Bridge which joined the Eastern and Western shores of the state. Below the wide expanse were sail boats, power pleasure cruisers, cargo ships and barges headed to their destinations. The water was choppy; the craft bobbed in the surf. The wind coming from the East caused the boats' sails and flags to flap in the breeze.

Don arrived in Baltimore later that day. The trip was just one hundred-fifty miles, with stops, about a four hour drive. Don had grown up close to the city. Although it had been thirteen years since he had lived in the area, he remembered it. Not much had changed. He drove into town heading for the Lord Baltimore Hotel where he had made reservations. By that time it was early evening.

After dinner, he decided to go up to Charles Street, where there were bars frequented by residents of the Mount Vernon area. Although it was several blocks, he decided that he needed a walk. As he proceeded up Charles Street the autumn sun was setting. The sky was painted with an orangish-red glow as the sunlight faded. Don walked past the Walters Art Gallery with its distinctive staircase and entrance. Further up the block he arrived at the Washington Monument. Built in 1829, it was an earlier version than the one in Washington, D.C. The smooth round stone structure stood one hundred seventy-eight feet high on a square base with an entrance. An adorned bronze door was flanked by two tall bronze torch lights. A cobblestone square surrounded the monument. Black wrought iron fencing surrounded the structure. A strip of manicured grass grew in front of the monument bordered by sidewalks where a reflecting pool mimicked the sunset. A fountain with a dancing nymph stood in front of the monument at the edge of the grass. George Washington was perched on top of the small round dome in a robe, like a Roman emperor. He was pointing into the distance as if to show the way. Don stopped and sat down on a concrete bench to gaze at the impressive structure thinking that he had forgotten how beautiful the city could be. Continuing to walk, he approached Mount Vernon, and continued past the Peabody Conservatory of Music on the corner to the right.

Two blocks up, he passed the Peabody Book Store, a coffee house with its door at the bottom of a stoop. Darkness had fallen and the lights illuminated the sign identifying the place. On the corner to the right and to the left were two upscale bars. Well lit outside, he approached The Charles on the right and walked in. The place was furnished with plush booths and mostly empty, red upholstered bar stools.

He introduced himself as an out of town visitor and casually asked about the local scene. He talked to several patrons with no luck. He had hoped that some information would fall into his lap as it had with Blackman. He tried not to think about those events and focus on his goal. After talking to several people at The Charles, he was not able to find anyone who had met him. On other nights that week he returned to the area and asked around at the Peabody Book Store.

The following Friday night, he went to Clyde's. He parked on the street around the corner. The bar was in the center of the room and took up most of the space. Tables on the right were full, crowded by chairs in between holding twenty-something customers. The bar was also packed. Music played loudly. Hall and Oates were singing *Sara Smile* as the place was filled with loud conversation and smoke. Don went to the bar and got a scotch. He stood to the side since there was nowhere to sit. He stood there for a while and decided to approach two women at the bar sitting on stools, apparently together for the evening.

"Hello… this is quite a crowd here tonight," Don said with a smile; the one that usually worked when being charming.

"Yeah, it usually is on a Friday night," said the attractive blond on the left, also stating the obvious.

"My name is Don."

"Hello," the blond said, smiling.

"Are you from the area?"

"Actually were from Pennsylvania," the blond said, showing an interest.

"We're students at Peabody," the other girl chimed in. "I'm Linda and this is Nancy."

She was less attractive than the blond but still pretty. They were both dressed in bell bottom jeans and Linda wore a peasant blouse with pink embroidered flowers on the front. Nancy wore a flowered shirt and a leather jacket with a short waist. The outfit was accentuated by a long beaded necklace and dangling earrings.

"I'm visiting from New York. I used to live in this area."

"Do you come to this place often?" Don asked, while thinking it was a typical pick up line.

"Yeah, pretty often," the blond said.

"I'm looking for a guy named John Weaver. He is about five feet ten with blond hair about collar length. Good looking, kinda' straight, a sharp dresser... obviously has money."

"We see some guys like that," said Linda.

"This guy has a small cyst next to his left eye."

"Oh yeah," Nancy said, remembering.

"There was a guy. We went out once. His name was John, but it was Webster. We met here and he asked me out to dinner about a month ago. We went back to his apartment on Mount Vernon Place."

"Oh really?" said Don with an interested tone.

"Well I liked him at first. He was quite charming but I was turned off. He was so arrogant. I guess he picked up on it because never called me after that."

"Yeah, we saw him here about two weeks ago and he didn't even speak... jerk," Linda added.

"I would like to get his address. We used to live together and he moved without saying anything. He owes me a lot of money on rent. It would really be a big help," Don said with that smile.

"Okay, why not," Nancy replied.

"Do you want my number too?" Nancy said, apparently taken with Don.

"Sure," Don replied, flattered that she had asked.

The next evening, Don drove to Weaver's address, or at least what he had hoped was the address, at 351 Mount Vernon Place. He parked his car on the street which sloped down just past the main entrance to the Peabody Conservatory. The full moon lit the street which was divided by a small park. A bronze sculpture of a naked little boy riding a dolphin was in the center casting a shadow on the walkway in front of it. The houses were quite old and stately. Built in the 1890's they were three stories high in a row with tall windows and high arching lit foyer entrances. Don sat on a concrete bench in the small island dividing the street. He was eager to get some answers. Earlier in the day he had purchased a, military issue, Remington .45 caliber semi- automatic handgun with a light brown grip. Don had learned to use a firearm during his teen years and practiced on a range from time to time.

At about ten o'clock he saw a man fitting Weaver's description. As the man was walking up the steps onto a small landing, Don quickly got out of the car. Unobserved, he crossed the street, skipped up the steps and stood directly behind him.

The man, dressed in a leather bomber's jacket and slacks opened the front door with his key. Don pushed him between the doors into the foyer. Don grabbed him from behind, twisted his arm from the back and stuck the forty-five against the back of his jacket.

"Are you Weaver," he demanded.

"Y-Yes," Weaver said, sounding startled.

"Let's go inside."

The two of them went down a hallway to the living room. Don shoved Weaver and he landed on an antique sofa.

"Who are you?" Weaver demanded.

Don held the forty-five on Weaver looking intensely into his eyes.

"You don't need to know. I know you are connected to Marna Anderson's murder and your involvement in the insider trading."

Weaver looked surprised. "How did you find me?"

"Never mind. You are going to tell me all about it." Don cocked the forty-five aiming it with the intention to intimidate. The gun wasn't loaded but Weaver didn't know that.

Weaver began to look nervous. Sweat was beginning to form on his brow. He ran his hands through his thick blond hair.

Don sat down in a velvet covered chair directly across from the couch.

"Why don't we start with the funds? How was Marna mixed up with it?"

"She gave us tips." Weaver's lips curled in a smirk.

"You're lying!"

"You wanted the truth!" Weaver exclaimed.

"I worked for Stern Investment Group and we were trading hedge funds. From contacts though attorneys at Wilson Jones, she was able to get information on upcoming mergers. In return she got a share of the profits. Blackman was a go between to disguise the operation."

"Why was she killed?"

"She's dead?... I...I...didn't know."

Don pointed the forty-five. "If you're lying...

"I swear, I swear, that's the truth."

"We made about four million on trades. I heard that she was going to the SEC."

"Maybe that's why she was killed."

"Who would do it?"

"I really don't know."

Feeling pressured, Weaver paused to think.

"Maybe a firm ... of professionals. They could have been hired to cover things up and minimize possible damage to the company."

The nightmare of the last year began to fall into place for Don. Although he could have been lying, Weaver's explanation made some sense. Marna's murder wasn't random and Don was almost run off the road to get rid of him.

There was no way that he could report what he had learned about Weaver without being implicated in Blackman's death.

"Don't tell anyone about our conversation," Don said angrily as he uncocked the forty- five and slowly lowered it.

"In the mean time I will keep tabs on you."

Don left the apartment and drove back to the hotel gratified that he was making progress but unsure about what to do next. He couldn't believe Marna was involved. The clues were there. He just ignored the possibility.

Don stayed around Baltimore for another week. The new medication was working wonderfully and he was sleeping better than he had in a long time. He visited the places he remembered from years past. He went to the Baltimore Zoo where he often spent Sunday afternoons with his family.

He drove to Woodlawn and went past the high school. A fenced in track/football field stood next to the road and the red brick buildings, their windows trimmed with green, were perched on the hill. He passed through the crossroads of town looking at the pharmacy, dry cleaner, little grocery/butcher shop, and a carry out restaurant on the corner, a beauty salon across the street and a bank on the opposite corner. As he drove, he passed two barber shops, a bakery, the elementary school with the Methodist church across the street, and a bar next door. He went past the Woodlawn Cemetery Lake where white swans swam. He remembered ice skating on the pond when it froze over in the winter. Fires in empty oil drums would burn on the banks to warm the skaters and boys played impromptu hockey games. He thought back to the hours he had spent riding his bike up and down the hills, exploring the cemetery and swinging on a Tarzan rope, skinny dipping in the stream. He then drove up the hill where his old house stood at the end of a now paved street. Woodlawn looked basically the same except for a recently built volunteer fire station.

CHAPTER NINETEEN

Don returned to New York. After bringing up his luggage and settled into his apartment, he fixed a drink and relaxed on the sofa and took a dose of Demerol. He reflected on the events of the last month and how he had gotten the answers he needed about Marna's murder. He hadn't dreamed she was involved. He wondered about the "security firm" and if they would again intimidate him. It was possible that this would happen since the case still had not been solved. He wasn't concerned, just mellow. Relaxed, he drifted off to sleep.

He awoke and saw Mary Saratt standing there in the middle of his living room. Her glowing face had a fixed expression in a half smile, like a Civil War era photo that glowed all over. Her brown hair was parted in the middle and tied back. He was wearing a light blue dress, long and full with three-quarter length sleeves. She had on a white blouse with frilly cuffs and a red scarf tied at the neck with a broach in the center of her white collar.

"Don, I know the truth," a woman's voice implored. Don remained seated on the couch staring in disbelief.

"Lincoln was betrayed. Go to my house and you will see."

The image disappeared. Don blinked his eyes and looked around. Did he have a dream? He wasn't sure.

As he shook off his sleepiness, he began to think about the boarding house in Washington D.C. Then he remembered that the residents of the house in Maryland had reported that strange noises and ghostly figures had appeared. It was reported that they saw a figure of Mary Saratt. Questions about her guilt in Lincoln's murder have remained. Her innocence is said to cause her spirit to linger in this world. Don couldn't imagine that Mary Saratt was haunting his living room! It must have been a very lucid dream. It disturbed him.

A week later, Don returned to work after a month of leave. He wasn't especially glad to be back. He was considering the possibility of giving up his job. His back wasn't getting any better despite the physical therapy he had received. The therapy helped for a while, but the pain returned and without the Demerol, he could not function. His life was moving in a different direction. The competitive pace of Madison Avenue no longer appealed to him. His focus was on his writing a book and he wanted to write in peace, away from all distractions.

After getting on the elevator, Don stood next to an attractive woman dressed in a dark blue business suit. He glanced at her trying not to be too obvious. Her light brown hair was long, down her back, curled at the end. Her large brown eyes stared at the numbers above indicating the floor. *She is a knockout. I wonder who she is.* The elevator stopped at Don's floor. The woman got out ahead of Don just as he made his move towards the open doors.

She walked down and adjoining corridor to the right and entered an office. *She works here, must be new.*

Don headed towards his office. He saw Judith in the hall.

"Hi Don, how was your trip?"

"I enjoyed spending time with my mother. I visited Baltimore and learned a lot," Don said looking toward the hall that the unknown woman had just entered.

Don was aware he was in a public area and began to look around. "Let's step into my office."

The two of them walked down the hall and through the reception area. They said hello to Paulette, who greeted Don and welcomed him back. They went into Don's office and he closed the door. Don sat in the chair at his desk and Judith sat across from him.

"I may have found out why Marna was murdered," Don said in a low tone as if he would be overheard.

"She was involved in insider trading."

"Insider trading, I don't believe it." Judith looked surprised.

"She knew too much and the partners got nervous."

"Don you have to report this," Judith said in a concerned tone.

"I can't. I don't have enough information yet. I'll need to wait until I have something more."

Judith could see that Don wasn't going to change his mind.

"How have you been sleeping," Judith inquired empathetically.

"I got a prescription which is helping me."

Don decided not to tell Judith that it was Quaaludes. They were getting a bad reputation and Don was satisfied with the drug's positive effect.

"I have been having strange dreams though," Don added trying not to look too concerned.

"What kind of dreams?"

"About Mary Saratt."

"Mary who?"

"You know from Lincoln's assassination," Don said, perturbed she didn't remember the connection.

"Her ghost is known to be wandering in Clinton, Maryland where she once lived with her husband. It used to be called Sarattsville until she was convicted of the assassination and it was changed."

"Really, is that what you are dreaming about?" Judith asked incredulously.

Don still wondered if it was a dream or a hallucination.

"Yes, and I have been thinking about possibly contacting her."

"Do you mean her ghost?"

"Yeah, the spirit of Mary Saratt. I have read about spiritualists, as they were called, trying to contact others beyond the grave. Mary Lincoln had tried to contact the spirits of her dead sons, Willie and Tad as well as her husband after his death. A more recent celebrated case was that of Houdini in the 1920's. His wife tried to contact him in the afterlife."

"Don, this whole thing seems a little far fetched." Judith was wondering if Don had lost his mind.

After Judith left his office, Don stopped in the reception area to talk to Paulette. He asked her about the unfamiliar woman on the elevator. Paulette said that she was a new employee of another firm who had begun the job when he was away on leave. Her name was Carol, an advertising executive. For the first time since Marna's death, Don was interested in a woman.

CHAPTER TWENTY

The weekend came and it was uneventful. The strange "dreams" had not occurred. Don decided to stay around the apartment, relax and rest. At times, his thoughts returned to Carol, the attractive woman he had seen at work. He wondered if she was seeing anyone.

He hadn't noticed any suspicious people following him and it appeared that after the encounter in Baltimore, they had backed off.

On Sunday, Don was relaxing in the living room reading the *New York Times*.

He spotted an article:

Medium Investigates Haunting of Plantation House in Maryland Selena Harris, a New York resident, made contact with the ghost of Elizabeth Calvert in an effort to remove her from the family home in Upper Marlboro, Maryland. The residence was built in 1725 by the Calvert family on the Mount Airy Plantation and was visited by George Washington several times.

The house was converted to a restaurant in 1903. Presidents Hoover, Taft, Coolidge and Wilson visited there. A renovation began in the 1930's and rumors of the house being haunted again circulated. In the 1930's the London Society for Psychical Research investigated the presence of Elizabeth Calvert, a descendent of the family who owned the estate. She was said to walk the halls of the mansion at night, searching for the family's missing jewels. There was said to be a ghost of a girl in a white dress who sometimes appeared. Also reported by guests, was an old unidentified woman who roamed from room to room at night waking the sleeping occupants. The house stood vacant for almost ten years after the State of Maryland purchased the plantation property and converted into the Rosaryville State Park. The house was purchased by the Kulla family and it was again opened as a restaurant. The house was restored and renovated, giving new life to the mansion and its ghostly inhabitants. Alarmed, the new owners requested that Mrs. Harris contact the spirit of Elizabeth Calvert and tell her to leave. The old woman also appeared during the séance and identified herself as Agnes. The woman had worked in the house as a maid and had died on the premises when she was accidentally trampled by horses drawing a carriage in front of the house.

This is very interesting, Don thought. He began to think about The Ghosts of Maryland book Kathy had given him in Gettysburg. He had found a person who may be able to help connect him with the spirit world. The two locations were both in the same area of Maryland, Prince George's County. Don had vaguely remembered that Mary's father, John had purchased his property there. He began to wonder if it was the same property. He got out some of the many books he collected about the period and began to cross reference the history. Don couldn't believe the coincidence. John Saratt had purchased two hundred fifty-seven acres of farmland from Charles B. Calvert, a descendent of Charles Calvert, fifth Lord Baltimore. It was part of the Mount Airy Plantation! The area was developed and became known as Sarattsville. By April 23, 1852, a two story frame building was under construction on the property. The structure would later become a tavern, polling place, as well as a home to John and Mary Saratt and their three children. It was there that John Wilkes Booth would stop on the night of April, 14 1865, during his escape from Washington after killing President Lincoln.

Don sat thinking about the coincidence of the two hauntings. Selena Harris was probably unaware of the unlikely connection of the two residences in history. He was going to contact Selena Harris and ask her to conduct a meeting at the Saratt House Museum which opened last year.

On Monday after work, Don left his office and walked down the hall toward the elevator. To the left, he saw the attractive brunette coming to the elevator from an adjoining hall. Don walked beside her toward the elevator.

"Hello," Don said smiling.

"Hello," the woman said in and interested tone.

"My name is Don. I work down the hall at Klein." Don extended his hand. Smiling, she clasped it in a polite manner.

"Good to meet you, my name is Carol Dowling." Her brown eyes met his briefly and Don could tell that she was interested in him.

"Do you work here in the building?" Don asked as if he were unaware.

"Yes, at Schumer and Associates."

"That is an excellent firm. What do you do there?"

"I'm in advertising."

"What a coincidence, so am I." Don stated the obvious because after all, this was Madison Avenue.

CHAPTER TWENTY ONE

Don called Kathy from his apartment. He hadn't talked to her since returning to New York from Springfield. The phone rang and answered in a cheerful tone.

"Hello."

"How are you sis?"

"Hi Donny. It's good to hear from you. How are you doing?"

"Ok...fine."

"Donny you sound a little out of it...like your sleepy."

"Well... I just woke up from a nap," Don lied.

"Tell me, how are you progressing with your book?"

"I am making excellent progress. Right now I am exploring how Mary Saratt fits into the equation."

Don did not tell Kathy about the dream, appearance, or whatever it was in his living room last week. Not wanting to involve Kathy, Don kept his discovery in Baltimore and the whole Wall Street scenario to himself.

"I'm thinking about trying to contact Mary's spirit."

"Her ghost roams the tavern," Kathy said jokingly, in a spooky manner.

Don chuckled.

I'm thinking about contacting a medium named Selena Harris. I read in the newspaper that she had been involved in a séance at the Mount Airy estate in the Upper Marlboro area of Maryland."

"Oh, really? The Saratt House is in the same area."

"That's right, isn't that a coincidence?"

"Selena Harris was able to contact Mary Calvert who roamed the house."

"Donny, do you really think that she can succeed in contacting Mary Saratt?"

"I am certain that if she has been successful in one case it is worth a try at the Saratt House and tavern. I have a strong feeling that she will appear and try to communicate with us."

"Donny, that would be great but I am not sure that I really have the same conviction you do about it."

"Kathy, we have done a lot together and this will be a great adventure."

"I'm game. Let me know if she is willing to try it and when you want to set it up. I will be there."

"Thanks sis, I knew that I could count on you."

"How is Mom doing?"

"She's fine. I had a great time when I visited her. After leaving Salisbury, I stayed in Baltimore a few days before returning to New York."

"You didn't call me," Kathy said scolding him.

"It was a brief trip and I was mainly interested in how Woodlawn looks after all these years." Don was becoming a good liar; the part of himself he had come to despise.

"Things look pretty much the same. It was interesting to revisit the memories from high school and our childhood."

Don changed the subject. "I've decided to leave my job at Klein."

He had given it a lot of thought. He just was not as interested in his career and as driven as he once was. Advertising was no longer his quest in life. Since Marna died, he has had a different perspective. With her death, part of him had been taken away—the edge he had as a top executive. The accident added to his new sense of mortality and an awareness of his direction in life.

Don had killed a man, even if by accident, and fled the scene. He continued to feel guilt about his actions. Sure, Blackman was probably guilty of arranging Marna's murder, but Don had killed in anger, even in self defense it was a piss poor excuse.

"Donny, are you sure that you want to leave? You have had such a great career."

"Kathy, I am not really physically able to do it like I could… and besides, I really want to pursue other things."

"Like your book?"

"Yeah."

"I really think you ought to reconsider but I know that when you have your mind set on things it is hard to dissuade you. When do you think it will be?"

"At this point I don't know," Don responded.

"Well Donny, it sounds like you made up your mind. Does Mom know?

"I haven't told her yet," Don said, sounding a little less assured.

"Well, don't be a stranger, call me."

"Sure sis."

After Don hung up with Kathy he called information to obtain Selena Harris' phone number. Fortunately, it was listed and he jotted it down on his pad with a pencil. He began to feel a little foolish as he dialed the number. He wondered if Judith and Kathy may be right—this could be a waste of time. Would she be interested in the Mary Saratt haunting as much as the Mary Calvert case? The phone rang at the other end with punctuated buzzes. The woman at the other end picked up the receiver.

"Hello," She said with a smooth alto pitched voice. "This is Selena Harris."

"Miss Harris, my name is Don Kendall," Don said trying to sound non-chalant.

"Mr. Kendall, what can I do for you?"

"I'm interested in holding a séance."

"May I ask, how have you heard about me?"

"I read about it in the *New York Times* and was hoping you would be interested."

"For what purpose would you like to hold a séance?"

"To contact the spirit of Mary Saratt at her house in Clinton Maryland."

"I was recently in Maryland…Upper Marlboro…at the Calvert Estate," she said, her voice indicating an increased interest."

"I know. That's where I got the idea to call you."

"Please fill me in. As I recall from my knowledge of the Lincoln assassination, Mary Saratt was hanged as a result of her role in the plot."

"That's right," Don said, glad that she understood the importance of the house.

"There have been reported events at the house which also served as a tavern. These observations by people who have lived there indicate that there may be spirits still in the house."

"That sounds interesting."

"What has been observed there?"

"The residents of the house saw a figure of Mary Saratt on a stairway. Others have reported hearing men's voices in the back of the house when no one was there. Employees of the museum located at the house and tavern have seen apparitions in Civil War period clothing."

"It sounds like more than one incidence of haunting. It is likely that there is something to it."

"Why don't I look at my schedule and call you back. Of course, you realize I charge a fee for my services."

"I assumed that you do," Don said. Don had expected to pay for her services. He was willing to, if it meant that there would be a possibility of understanding the strange happenings at the house and contacting Mary.

"I would suggest that you have at least two other people to participate in a séance. It seems to get better results."

Don had already gotten Kathy to agree but had to think of someone else. Judith seemed the logical choice. On the other hand, she was too cerebral and was not likely to believe in spirits from the other side. Paulette seemed a more likely person.

"Selena, I'm glad that you are interested in the case," Don said with enthusiasm.

"I will look forward to hearing from you soon."

"Sure, I'll call you this week." Don hung up the phone excited about Selena's interest.

He began to think that perhaps she needed to make some money or further build her reputation. Don refused to believe that he was being led on. Whatever her motives, she had shown success in the past. That's what mattered.

CHAPTER TWENTY TWO

Detective Sanderson didn't like unsolved murders. The Anderson case had been on his mind for more than a year. It stuck in his craw. The insider trading had to be the key to it all. He had gotten some information from the Securities and Exchange Commission; the bastards were typical federal bureaucrats who guarded their case like it was their little sister's virginity.

Marna Anderson was a major player. She had provided inside information to the brokers making the deals. Although it hadn't happened yet, arrests were about to be made. Dan Blackman was not a major player, was on the periphery, connected, but not directly involved in the trading.

When the arrests came down someone was going to talk. Then he could get to the bottom of this.

Don continued to worry about his implication in the death of Blackman. Strangely, there was nothing else in the news about it. He knew that he would get a call sooner or later. Although the planning of the séance and his relationship with Carol were effective distractions, it played on his mind.

There was also a strange silence in the media about the insider trading scheme. There were a few reports in the newspaper and on television about the "continuing" investigation that no one would comment on.

He was going to leave town before it all came crashing down on him. He had to finalize his plans. Wyoming was a place that he had often thought about and had read up on. It was a place that had flat, wide open spaces and wonderful scenery with beautiful mountains and lakes. He decided that he would travel the National Lincoln Highway across the country. There, he could write his book without any distractions.

He had shopped around for vans at some dealerships in the area. He had decided on a Chevy Sportvan. This would be perfect for the trip. It was fully loaded. The van had a six cylinder engine, air conditioning, tape deck, and power steering. There were windows in the two rear doors which opened on each side. A spare tire was mounted on the right rear door. There was a sliding door with two small windows on the passenger's side of the vehicle. The driver's side also had an extra window for great visibility.

When the time was right, he would be leaving. He knew that before then, he had to bring Marna's killers to justice.

CHAPTER TWENTY THREE

It was Thursday. Don saw Carol again leaving work, this time on the elevator and he struck up a conversation. She looked more stunning that he remembered upon first meeting her a week ago. She was dressed in a light gray form fitting pin stripe pants suit. She had on a light blue blouse, her ample bust was apparent under the buttoned double breasted coat. Her brown hair was mid length, falling to her shoulders, a color reminiscent of Marna's.

"Hi, how are you?" Don said.

"Going down?"

"Yes, to the lobby," Carol said smiling, her intelligent brown eyes gazing at him. He looked at her and smiled as he pressed the elevator button.

There was an obvious attraction.

"How's business at Schumer," Don said to make conversation.

"Why…are you trying to size up the competition?" she kidded. Don smiled.

"Your name is Carol, right? "

"Yes it is," she said in a lilting voice.

"Yours is Don, right?"

"Yes it is," Don said mimicking her. Carol smiled and chuckled.

The elevator arrived at the lobby and the bell dinged. Carol stepped out first, Don followed.

"Listen Carol.... would you join me for lunch tomorrow?"

"I would be delighted," Carol replied in an interested tone.

"I will drop by the office about twelve-thirty tomorrow. Sound good?"

"Okay, I will see you then."

Don was surprised with himself. He had asked her to lunch on the spur of the moment. He didn't think that it would occur so naturally, without hesitation, just as it had for Marna. He really hadn't had much female companionship other than with Judith at lunch over the last year. He found Carol quite interesting. The attraction was there. He hoped that he would have something in common with Carol since they were in the same line of work.

Don took a cab back to his apartment. He fixed himself a scotch, took four Demerol and sat back in his Lazeboy chair. The Demerol took effect immediately in combination with the scotch. Over time, he had taken them more often and increased the number. He feared that he was developing dependency. He had convinced his doctor that he needed the medication and he kept writing the prescriptions. He was still taking the Quaaludes at night for sleep but had managed to keep the dose low. He was tired of lying to everyone to disguise his level of use to function. Ashamed, he couldn't bring himself to expose it. He always considered himself too strong morally and too successful to be an addict.

CHAPTER TWENTY FOUR

It was a bright, sunny day. A breeze brushed his face and teased his hair as he walked from his cab to the sleek office building.

Don was anticipating his lunch with Carol today. She was an interesting woman, and attractive. He wasn't sure where this was going but being in her company made him feel good and the possibility of a romantic relationship was intriguing. He had to get over any comparisons to Marna and let things occur naturally.

When he arrived on his floor, he greeted Paulette as he walked in and closed his office door. He began work on the ongoing project which was now taking months to complete. The morning passed and the lunch hour approached.

Don met Carol in the lobby and the two walked to Michael's Café. They strolled to the café, smiling as they talked. Don noticed a dark blue Crown Victoria parked on the opposite side of Madison Avenue. Given his previous experience, he was at first alarmed. *You are really losing it Don. How many blue Crown Vics do you think are in New York City? It doesn't mean anything.*

They continued to walk until they came to the restaurant. The place was busy with the lunch crowd but they found a table toward the back of the small place. They sat facing each other, Don looking out the large window toward the street. The car was still there. Don continued to talk to Carol trying not to think about it.

"Hungry?" Don inquired.

"I'm famished, I skipped breakfast today," Carol admitted.

"Well, I'm hungry too," Don said, as he looked at the menu the waitress had brought.

The waitress re-appeared and they both ordered sandwiches and a bowl of soup.

Thinking that they shared that in common, Don struck up a conversation about business.

"Have you been busy at work?"

The waitress returned and gave them each their orders.

"Yes, very much," Carol said in between bites.

"We are working on a new account with Chevrolet. Imported auto sales are beginning to overtake domestic brands and this campaign is an effort to get consumers back."

"I guess that I am one of those people since I bought a Nissan," Don said smiling ironically.

"You see! Our ad campaign is important to our clients."

"How long have you been working at Schumer?"

"Almost a year."

"It's amazing that I have not seen you."

"After graduating from Fordham University, I have been working in New York for a couple years until this opportunity came up."

"I'm glad it did."

"What have you been working on?" Carol asked.

"I have been working on a project that isn't really too exciting," Don said absent mindedly as he gazed out the window.

"I have an account with Volvo Canada that I am working on right now."

The Crown Vic was still there. A man sat in the driver's seat smoking a cigarette, killing time. Don again resisted the urge to jump to conclusions. He hadn't been bothered for months by these men who seem to think he knows something.

Don was growing tired of the office talk and decided to change the subject.

"Do you want to come to a séance?"

"A séance? Why?" Carol said, surprised by sudden question.

"I am writing a book about Abraham Lincoln and it is part of my research. Mary Saratt was known to be part of the plot to abduct and to later kill him. The séance is to try and contact her spirit and to possibly learn more about her involvement."

"I have to admit... this would be an unusual date, she said laughing slightly... but I would find it very interesting. The occult has been a fascination of mine since I was in my teens."

"Great," Don said enthused.

He looked out the window. The car was gone. He still wondered if he was being watched. *It is probably a coincidence*, he thought.

They finished lunch and walked back to the office. The sun shone down reflecting on the numerous glass windows of the building. It was a pleasant enough lunch but Don wondered if he had come off as aloof and a little odd to Carol.

When they reached the floor they got off the elevator. They paused for a minute.

"I enjoyed the lunch and your book sounds interesting," Carol said.

"I would like to do it again."

"Sure," Don said, his concerns a bit allayed.

"I'll call you at the office."

When Don returned to his office the phone rang. He picked up the receiver. Paulette's voice chirped.

"Call on line one."

"Hello Don, this is Selena Harris."

"Selena, it's good to hear from you."

"I have selected a date for the meeting."

"Okay… when?" Don said excitedly.

"Saturday, September twenty-sixth would be a good day for me."

"That looks good," Don said, consulting his calendar.

"Where do we meet?"

"I think the best place is at the Saratt House in Clinton Maryland. Meet me there with the other participants in the séance."

"Sounds good…what time?"

"After dark…let's make it eleven o'clock. Make arrangements with the museum to use the building after it closes."

Don thought that it would take some doing but he could arrange it, even if he had to invite a Prince Georges County Department of Parks employee. In his past experience, he had known someone who may be able to help him.

"If we are able to contact her spirit I want you to ask her two important questions," Don insisted.

"Sure. That won't be a problem. We can talk about that later. Alright then, it sounds like it's about set. I'll call you when we get closer to the date to confirm."

On the way out of the office Don saw Paulette in the reception area. He decided to ask her about the séance.

"Hey Paulette, would you join me in a fun activity next month?"

Paulette turned from the desk where she was typing.

"Sure… what do you have in mind," she said, always ready to try something exciting.

"I am having a séance."

"Do you mean like the movie I saw on T.V.?"

"What movie?" Don said, not knowing what she was taking about.

"It was called The Haunting, starring Julie Harris. She is part of a group trying to contact spirits in this haunted place called Hill House. People had died accidentally and someone committed suicide. Her friend, Claire Bloom is a clairvoyant who helps her. All kinds of weird things happened. It was pretty scary."

Don was amused and smiled.

"Well Paulette… there may be some strange things that will happen. We may see apparitions."

"Do you mean dead people walking around? …Ghosts?"

Don laughed. "Yeah, there might be something like that, or voices."

"Don, you can count me in. That sounds like a once in a life-time experience."

CHAPTER TWENTY FIVE

The days in September passed. Throughout the past two weeks, Don had gone out on other dates with Carol. They went to some restaurants, saw A Chorus Line, and went out to lunch at Michael's. They had become good friends. Although attracted to her, he did not have the same feelings as he had for Marna. The wound left by her death had not fully healed and memories still lingered. The comparisons of Carol to Marna were inevitable. That wasn't fair to Carol, but just the same, it was a fact.

In the early evening, Don, Carol and Paulette drove to Clinton Maryland. As they traveled down I-95 the sun set with orange and grayish blue streaks in the sky as darkness came. As they drove south of Baltimore around Washington D.C., Don began to reflect on the events of Lincoln's assassination and Mary Saratt's fate. Mary had known Booth after she had rented the tavern and ran a boarding house in Washington. Her son, John was taken with Booth who was a superstar in his day. Mary was known as a "Confederate sympathizer" and, in fact, had owned several slaves. At first, plans were made to kidnap Lincoln and several items were stored at the Saratt House including some rope and rifles. At Mary's boarding house in Washington, and later at the tavern adjoining the house, a group plotted the kidnapping and later, the assassination. After Booth shot Lincoln, he headed south to Sarattsville, winding up at the house to retrieve two carbines, drink, rations and some field glasses. Booth had reportedly asked Mary to deliver a package containing field glasses for him at the house. Mary was accused of making arrangements for Booth by getting the items ready for Booth's escape. Mary was tried and hung along with the other conspirators. The extent of her guilt has been questioned ever since.

After getting on Route 5, they saw the exit for Clinton. As he got off the exit Don saw a well lit brown and white sign: **The Saratt House Museum.**

Woodyard Road was the main drag through town. Don imagined it had once been a rural crossroads with businesses of a small town—a tailor, lawyer, butcher, the Saratt Tavern and Boarding House, with a blacksmith and livery stable across the road. The two lane road was busy with traffic. All types of chain restaurants advertised with bright signs and gas stations stood on the corners. Don followed the road until he saw another small sign with an arrow indicating the direction of the museum. They came to Brandywine Road, and made a left turn toward the site.

He had called Kathy a few weeks earlier excitedly telling her about the plans for a séance with Selena, and she agreed to meet him at the museum. Don had called the Prince George's County Department of Parks explaining that he was a historian writing a book about Lincoln, Saratt and the strange happenings at the tavern. This, of course, was bending the truth, but was not an outright lie. In part, his book was going to be about her. He dropped the name of his contact with the Saratt Society and managed to obtain permission to use the museum a couple of hours after the museum had closed.

As they turned onto Brandywine Road, it was dark. The shadows of residential houses were barely visible in the dim light from their porches. On the left was a fence and a barely noticeable sign next to the road and the small entrance to the now closed house. It was as Don had imagined from photographs: a two story clapboard structure with nine windows on the front, shutters on each window, two side windows and a smaller attached section with a chimney. There was a side entrance with a ramp leading to the tavern. A porch-like roof covered the entrance. Evident in the headlights was a **Saratt Tavern** sign suspended from a small front porch post. A parking lot was to the right of the house as they pulled in. The dark silhouette of the house stood to the left of them with a path leading up to the front door.

Kathy was waiting in her Chevette, and Selena pulled up in her car a few minutes later. It was ten-thirty. The woman from the museum was waiting in front to let them in. Only open during the day, the museum had no lighting. Selena introduced herself in the parking lot before proceeding towards the house. Guided by flashlights, they walked down the path towards the house—a small sign announced **Tours.**

Selena Harris was a short woman in her fifties. Her graying hair was long and drawn back off her face revealing deep lines in her forehead. Her brown, penetrating eyes projected a worldly countenance as she introduced herself to Don and the others. Don noticed, as she walked toward the house, her posture was stooped as if carrying the weight of a hundred souls.

The group entered the front door. Holding her flashlight, the historical society guide directed them to the parlor directly on the right. The room was furnished with period furniture. It was evident from the furnishings that Mary Saratt had all the comforts of the time. In the middle of the room was a tea table of dark mahogany with scalloped edges and large carved legs with clawed feet. A lit hurricane lamp sat in the center. In the corner was a love seat with a dark green winged back trimmed in mahogany. There was a small spinet piano with a flat top in the opposite corner, music propped on the music stand. Another lit oil lamp emitted light in the corner. Wood framed paintings adorned the amber walls. A tan and dark blue patterned rug adorned the wood floor. A fireplace painted black was to the left of the room with a long gold framed mirror above the hearth. Candles, decorative china vases, sea shells and framed pictures sat on the mantle. Five chairs were arranged around the table for the séance. The museum escort said she would return at twelve-thirty and left.

Holding a candle in the darkness, Selena walked around the house, slowly walking up the stairs and to the back bedroom on the second floor. She stopped at times and felt the walls to tune in to any feelings that the house evoked. She slowly walked down the stairs turning to the back of the house where the kitchen, guest and family dining rooms were located. Since the adjoining tavern was not an area known to have otherworldly activity, she did not explore it. The rest of the group stood in the parlor respecting her space and allowing her to explore and sense any activity.

Selena returned to the parlor after several minutes. The group sat in the chairs with the table in the center. Don sat across from Selena with Carol on the right of him and Kathy on the left. Paulette sat next to Selena also opposite Don. The group held hands and intently listened as Selena spoke.

"I sense the presence of several entities. There are several men and a woman. I am not getting too much about the reason for the men not passing into the next world. Perhaps they were boarders who were killed in the Civil War but Mary continues to stay in this house to resolve the misfortunes in her life."

"Who do you sense is the strongest presence?" Don said expectantly.

"It is definitely Mary Saratt. I think it would be possible to communicate with her if we concentrate and try to create a link." Selena paused and closed her eyes in deep concentration.

"Mary... if you are here, please move something... make a sound... so that we know you are present."

The room was perfectly silent and still. The candles burned in the dark room illuminating the walls behind them, the table and the faces of those present. They sat for what seemed like an hour intently listening.

Suddenly, the candles flickered, as if a breeze were passing though the room. Up to that point there had been no draft in the room and the temperature was cool but comfortable. The faces of the group began to show a growing apprehension. As he waited and listened, Don noticed that the temperature in the room was dropping. He could see his breath.

"I feel a strong presence," Selena said as she sat with her eyes closed.

"Mary, are you there? It is safe to communicate with us. We are friends. Further reveal your presence."

Don heard the light tapping of footsteps decending the second floor staircase and coming into the room.

"Do you hear that?" He asked Selena.

"Yes, I hear it," Kathy responded excitedly before Selena could say anything.

The footsteps led into the parlor but the sound stopped by the fireplace. A vase on the mantle moved and tipped off the edge, crashing on the floor, shattering into pieces. Both Paulette and Kathy flinched. A few minutes passed.

"Mary, we are aware of your presence," Selena stated.

"Reveal yourself to us."

The group waited. Mary Saratt's image appeared standing next to the fireplace. It was transparent, but faintly there.

"There she is!" Paulette excitedly whispered.

The image was older and looked more haggard than the painting in the hallway that depicted Mary. She was dressed as women did of the time: a full blue, ankle-length dress, with three-quarter length sleeves and a white, long sleeved bodice fastened at the neck and held in place by a broach. Her hair was tied back with a scarf. The image faded in and out like a television not quite picking up reception. Don stared in disbelief at the image. Was it a dream this time? Don wasn't sure.

"Mary… we are glad you are with us," Selena said.

"Will you answer questions that we have always been wondering?" The apparition looked straight ahead… Selena paused.

"Did you know Mary Todd Lincoln?"

The apparition of Mary nodded her head.

"Was she involved in the plans to abduct her husband?"

The image remained motionless, as if not understanding the question or not wanting to respond. Then it nodded slightly.

Selena paused for a few moments to reflect on the next question.

"Are you guilty of plotting to kill President Lincoln?" The image flickered, faded and disappeared.

"Mary... Mary, are you still here?" Selena implored.

The group sat and waited. The room slowly returned to its previous temperature.

"Mary...please return to us."

As the group waited for several minutes, there was no response.

"I think she is gone," Selena said.

"My god," Don said as he let out a breath. "That was unbelievable."

After the séance was over, the participants talked in hushed tones outside the house for a few minutes, all stunned in disbelief. Don said goodbye to Selena, gave her a check and thanked her. Kathy hugged Don and got in her car and drove away.

Don, Carol and Paulette drove back to New York. They said little, but Don was ecstatic. Paulette kept saying "awesome" over and over. As they drove back into the city, Carol sat next to Don silently as Don kept talking about the evening. They agreed to meet for lunch on Monday. He dropped her off at her apartment and they kissed good night.

CHAPTER TWENTY SIX

The following Monday, Carol waited for Don at Michael's. Don arrived late. He looked disheveled. His hair was unkept, he had not shaved and although clean, his clothes appeared rumpled.

"Don you look horrible," Carol said a little shocked.

"Well... I have had some trouble sleeping, but I have been so excited about the happenings at the Saratt House that I don't care. I now have the basis for my book about Abraham Lincoln's assassination."

Don's eyes looked bloodshot and his face had a crazed look. He spoke in rapid sentences.

"I could write the most ground breaking book about Lincoln to date. My theory about the conspiracy is different than any that I have heard or read about. You see, there is life beyond the grave. Mary showed me that. I believe there is another dimension, a spiritual world and I want to lead others to it. I could be a prophet of men."

Carol sat in disbelief. Don looked like a totally different person. He had an almost delusional quality about him. Was he high ... on drugs? She could understand his enthusiasm. She was there and had witnessed the same thing at the Saratt House. Perhaps he is just reacting to the bizarre events. A prophet of men? That did seem delusional.

"I have been thinking about going to Wyoming to write my book. There I can attract a group of believers who will listen to my message."

A group...it sounds more like a cult, Carol thought.

"Wyoming... why Wyoming?"

"It is a quiet, serene place, where I can find peace. I often think about the mountains and clear lakes."

Don's fatigued eyes looked off into the distance as he spoke.

"The air is so crisp and clean ... there is no one around for miles."

Don knew that he had to get away. He was ultimately going to be arrested for Blackman's murder if the "firm" of professional killers didn't get him first. Was he really getting in deep with the pain killers and losing his grip? Was he delusional? Perhaps.

As they ate lunch, Don couldn't reveal to Carol the underlying reason for his behavior. He nibbled on his sandwich, not really having an appetite. He began to think for whatever reason, he was losing it. Perhaps it was because he had stopped taking the Quaalude medication. Ever since then, he couldn't sleep and felt frazzled; out of touch with reality. That could explain his state of mind.

CHAPTER TWENTY SEVEN

Detective Sanderson finally got more information about the insider trading scheme which involved Marna Anderson and Dan Blackman. The Feds had finally provided him something with prodding and with the right connections. Indictments of two former Stern Investments hedge fund managers were being prepared. Blackman was an outsider who knew them all and had involved Anderson in the insider trading scheme. Several funds traded by Stern were purchased with the knowledge of upcoming mergers and acquisitions, thus giving them forewarning of their increase in value. The men, Matthew Simms and Ralph Augustine, were about to be arrested.

Don Kendall must have known about Blackman's connection to the scheme. Witnesses had identified someone fitting Kendall's description at the scene. The only thing left was to call him in for questioning.

Don returned to his apartment after leaving Michaels Café. He had no intention of going to work. He hadn't talked to Judith in some time and decided to call her to tell her about his decision to leave Klein. He dialed Judith's number.

"Klein and Associates," Judith said when she answered.

"Hi. Judith, this is Don."

"Hi, Don."

"I heard about the séance. Paulette came in babbling about Mary Saratt's ghost. Come on. Did that really happen?"

"Yes it did. At least I think it did." Don said in defense of Paulette.

"Okay… if you say so."

Don was really glad that he didn't ask her to participate.

He decided to come to the point. "Judith, I won't be in to work today. As a matter of fact, I may not be back at all."

"Don, are you serious? Aren't you going to give them some notice… resign?"

"I am actually going to send something. In the meantime, I am going to take a leave of absence. But I am relying on you to tell them," Don said confidently.

"What are you going to do?" Judith said flabbergasted.

"I am going to Jackson Wyoming to write the book I have talked about for years. I have made plans," Don lied.

"Don, I think you should reconsider, but it sounds like your mind is made up."

"By the way, a Detective Sanderson called you and left a message to call him back."

A chill ran through Don. He knew that the detective might be putting two and two together. It was likely that the insider trading investigation was moving forward. The next step for Detective Sanderson would be to discover the connection Blackman had to the case and that Don had been at his apartment. It was a matter of time before he would be implicated.

"Thanks for relaying the message," Don said nonchalantly.

"I have the number. I'll call to see what he has for me. Judith, don't worry I'll be fine. This will be a new phase of my life… one I have been looking forward to for a long time."

"I know that writing this book is a dream of yours. I hope that all goes well," Judith said encouragingly.

"Thanks. I will write to you and let you know how I am doing."

"Okay… good luck."

CHAPTER TWENTY EIGHT

Don had looked in the newspaper and on television about the insider trading scandal. There was nothing for weeks—but this week he saw a headline:

Two Stern Investment Group Hedge Figures Indicted

Two men, Matthew Simms and Ralph Augustine were arrested and arraigned yesterday on nine counts of securities fraud, wire fraud and conspiracy. They are also charged with employing their security firm to cover up the scheme. Simms was arrested at his home in Long Island and Augustine at his New York City apartment. Pending their trial, the two men are expected to be released on bail tomorrow.

He was going to take the opportunity to question them and find out who this "security firm" was and give Sanderson the evidence he needed to convict them of murder.

Don spent some time packing up his apartment. He had given notice to the landlord that it would be his last month and told him to forward anything to his mother's address in Salisbury, until he found another place to live. He made arrangements for his furniture to be stored. After selling most of his stock investments, and making a substantial deposit into his checking account, he paid cash for the Chevy van he had picked out a few months ago. He was ready to go. He had one more thing to do—call his sister.

The phone rang and Kathy's voice came on the line.

"Hi Sis," Don said trying to sound positive.

"Donny, how are you?"

"I'm doing OK. Hey… I have some good news. I am finally going out to Wyoming to write that book I have been talking about for years. I am really excited about getting started and will be leaving this week."

Don hated lying to her but did not want to involve her in this.

"You really made your mind up quickly. Are you going to Jackson as we have talked about?"

"Yeah, I have been thinking about it for a long time and now I am ready. I going to resign from my job and I have given up my apartment. I even bought a new van. You would like it. It's a sporty model and perfect for a cross-country trip."

"Donny, are you sure you want to do this? It is really a drastic decision."

"I really feel that this is the time."

"Well Donny, it sounds like your really leaving," Kathy said more convinced.

"I really am," Don said with conviction.

"Sis, I have to go. I will write you to let you know how I am doing and will call you after I get there."

"Okay, Donny. Have a good trip, and be careful."

Detective Sanderson had not been able to reach Kendall. He had tried at the office and his home. There were several unanswered questions. He rode to Don's Park Avenue apartment but did not find him there. He had moved out. He decided to question Simms and Augustine to learn about their knowledge of the murder. After all, he had jurisdiction.

Sanderson pulled up in his unmarked white cruiser at the house of Matthew Simms in the suburban Long Island town of Bay Shore. The town was a shore community along Long Island Sound next to Fire Island National Seashore. The area was a mix of new houses and older dwellings. Simms house was a brick Georgian style ten bedroom with a large lawn, high fences and a security gate. When entering the driveway, Sanderson pushed the speaker button next to the gate with his elongated finger and announced his intention to speak to the owner.

Sanderson was buzzed in and drove up to the front door. He got out and walked to the entrance. He had on his favorite gray suit and a dark blue tie. The door immediately opened. A smiling Asian woman who was apparently the house keeper greeted him.

"I am here to see Mr. Simms. He is expecting me," the detective said, not feeling like smiling back.

Sanderson held up his wallet containing his identification and badge.

"I will let him know you are here."

"Thank you."

Sanderson entered the den, unbuttoning his overcoat. Simms walked in looking a little annoyed. He was a tall man in his early forties with a full head of curly brown hair with graying temples.

"You must be detective Sanderson."

"That's right," he said showing his NYPD badge.

"I have already had plenty of investigators questioning me about my finances but what's this about?"

"There was a young woman, Marna Anderson... killed in Chelsea over a year ago. Did you know her?"

Simms paused to choose his words carefully.

"I never heard of a woman named Marna Anderson."

"I know that I am in trouble due to my business transactions but do you really think I had anything to do with a murder?"

Sanderson looked at his suspect intently. His wrinkled brow furrowed. He did not believe Simms.

"You had a security firm who you hired to protect yourself and your partner. Could they be involved?"

"I guess it is a possibility. I assure you that I had no knowledge of anyone being murdered."

Sanderson had to accept his explanation. He had no proof at this point except that the both Simms and Anderson were implicated in the insider trading.

"Eventually it will be clear as to your exact relationship with Ms. Anderson and after all the facts are in—I am going to charge you and your associates with this senseless crime." The detective turned toward the door.

"I will be in touch," he stated, while exiting the house to the front porch.

Instinct developed through years of experience told the detective that Simms was involved. He may not have planned the murder but was covering it up.

Sanderson left the house thinking that he had to question the other suspects and perhaps he could persuade them to offer information for a deal.

CHAPTER TWENTY NINE

Don sat in the upscale bar and grille in upper Manhattan nursing a scotch. He sat at the bar looking at the television mounted on the wall facing him. Cigarette smoke drifted though the air and insulted Don's nostrils. He turned slightly on his stool, ignoring it.

The news broadcast about the arrest the previous day of Simms and Augustine flashed on the screen. The footage showed Simms and the arresting officers speeding off in an unmarked police car from his Long Island home.

Don began to think about the chain of events leading to Marna's murder. Simms or Augustine knew something about it since they had hired a security firm. He began to think about Simms. He could find the house. He had been in that area a few times to visit Madison Avenue friends and had a good idea where the house was. He had to go there to question Simms and get to the truth.

The Chevy Sportvan headed on the Long Island Freeway toward Bay Shore. The van was mostly metallic grey with a bright orange stripe separating the upper third of the van from the black lower half where the wheel wells, recessed chrome wheels, and the wide truck tires were located.

As Don drove onto the island there was a breeze blowing off the sound. The landscape of sea oats, wildflowers and bushes came into view. He popped in the Neil Young **Harvest** cassette he had taken out of the Nissan when he traded it in—the smashed in side panel, the bent front and damaged back fenders included.

Heart of Gold began to play. Neil Young's lonely voice began to whine about being a miner for a heart of gold. The music continued at a medium, punctuated pace.

Don began to relax. He had been restless and irritable since quitting the Quaaludes. He had made the decision after his lunch in the café with Carol. It was getting out of hand. He was still having some stomach cramps and mild shaking in his hands. He was tired and his mind wandered. He was extremely on edge and did not trust his senses.

Don entered the neighborhood of Bay Shore. He saw a car enter the road from the left and was traveling behind him. In the rear view mirror he saw a midnight blue Crown Victoria with two passengers. Don tensed up. He studied the driver's side rear view mirror. The car was moving in. Don squinted, and widened his eyes, not sure that what he had seen was real. He increased his speed to provide distance from the Crown Vic. Don had his loaded forty-five under the driver's seat in case he needed it. He leaned over and searched for the weapon with his right hand under the seat, holding the wheel with his left, feeling for it in a panic.

His irritability continued and in fact, increased. The calming effect of the music no longer helped. The next track came on the cassette player. He didn't dare turn his attention to the cassette player to turn it off. The song had a stronger beat and Don's pulse quickened. As the Crown Vic began closing on him he found the gun and pulled it from under the seat. Memories of his horrible experience driving to Springfield gripped him. He wasn't going to let them ram him again.

While holding the wheel with both hands, he pulled back the slide cocking mechanism of the forty-five and wound down the driver's side window. Looking back, he stuck it out the window in the direction of the Crown Vic's grille and fired. The scent of burnt powder drifted into Don's face. The shot hit the large grille and the car swerved. Now alerted, the car lunged further forward.

Don became angrier, his face red and contorted. The music pulsated—guitars and a piano punctuating the lilting beat. He looked in the large side mirror, turned again, and fired twice, one bullet missing wildly and the other hitting the windshield of the Crown Vic. The car lost control and swerved to the left, going into a ditch. The Crown Vic quickly regained control and re-entered the road, its tires muddy. Don continued to drive at a suicidal speed looking back at the menacing vehicle pursuing him. A gun popped three times and a bullet hit the back of the van making a dull thud. Don returned fire—this time, a lucky shot hit and blew out the right front tire of the Crown Vic. The car swerved and braked abruptly, its tires squealing. Don slammed on his brakes, left the van in the middle of the road and jumped out. He ran toward the Crown Vic like a linebacker charging an opposing ball runner. The two men were somewhat shaken up by the abrupt jolt and were slow in getting out of the car. Don was there with the forty-five trained on them before they could react.

"Get your god-dammed hands up!" Don demanded. The two men complied, looking a little surprised. Don was beginning to calm down and recognized one of the men.

"You...Weaver!" Don shouted.

"I remember you from Baltimore. You son of a bitch! Which one of you killed my girlfriend?"

Don pointed the gun at the two men. He had never been so angry. His hands shook as his finger tightened on the trigger.

The other man, stocky with muscular shoulders made a move and put his hand inside the breast of his coat. Don fired. The gun punctuated and kicked in his hand. The man, hit in the shoulder fell in the road.

"Who are you working for?" Don spat the question. Weaver hesitated.

Bleeding, the other man was on the ground writhing and moaning.

"Tell me or I'll blow you away."

"Simms hired us to keep tabs on her. We went to her apartment to warn her not to tell anyone about the information she gave Blackman. We didn't kill her...we just wanted to scare her."

"I don't believe you. I want you to take me to Simms house and we will have a talk."

Don pointed the forty-five and waved it.

"Walk toward the van."

Weaver walked toward the middle of the road towards the van with Don following. Suddenly, a light blue Buick sedan pulled up from behind them and squealed its brakes. Don broke for the van as bullets whizzed over his head. He jumped in and hit the accelerator. Looking in the rear view mirror, he saw Weaver jump back into the Crown Vic. The Buick followed him and they kept coming.

Don then heard a siren. He looked back and an unmarked white police car was in pursuit. The little portable bubble light was pulsating on top of the car.

Sanderson...Don thought. *It had to be.*

CHAPTER THIRTY

Sanderson had driven from Simms house when he heard gunshots popping in rapid succession. He accelerated after turning off the street that he was traveling on and at a distance, he saw the Chevy van in the middle of the road. The Crown Vic sedan was also stopped there with both its front doors open. A man was off to the side of the road writhing in pain. As Sanderson rushed toward the scene, Kendall jumped in and the van took off.

As Sanderson got closer, a man jumped into the Crown Vic and took off, limping down a narrow side street, sparks flying from the front end. A light blue Buick LeSabre screeched off chasing the van. Sanderson quickly pulled over to the side of the road and got out of his cruiser. He pulled his Colt .38 police revolver from the side holster under his coat and approached the wounded man.

"Are you okay?

"I'm going to live," he finally answered.

"Can you control the bleeding until help arrives?" The man was only wearing a tee-shirt and had used his shirt for a tourniquet.

Sanderson stood over the wounded man with his thirty-eight still trained on him.

"Who do you work for?"

"We are doing security for Stern."

"Do you mean the company that Matthew Simms works for?"

"Yes."

"I have some questions for you. For now, consider yourself under arrest." He was in no condition to go anywhere. Sanderson was not concerned that he would try to flee.

"Don't move until help arrives. A police officer will be here."

Sanderson got back in his unmarked car. He accelerated in pursuit of the two vehicles. He had to forget about the Crown Vic for now.

Don continued to drive as the Neil Young song continued to play.

Hearing the siren, the light blue sedan slowed. Don saw his chance and took an abrupt right. The van swerved and upended on two wheels but did not capsize. He headed for the Long Island Freeway. The van was pushing ninety. As he drove, Don looked back for anyone in pursuit. The other vehicle wasn't there. Don breathed a sigh of relief. He nervously checked his mirror again. So far, no Buick. The Neil Young tape ended and the music stopped.

Slowing down, he began to relax and turned onto Route 27, a less traveled road. When coming to the signs, he headed south entering I-84 blending in with the other cars. The traffic was heavy. He accelerated, exiting Long Island.

Sanderson quickly caught up to the Buick. He continued to pursue it. The Buick accelerated to up to one hundred miles per hour. Sanderson kept pace and got on his radio, calling for backup.

CHAPTER THIRTY ONE

Detective Sanderson continued to pursue the speeding vehicle and was joined by two NYPD squad cars on Long Island Expressway and though the Queens Mid-Town Tunnel. The Buick continued to travel at suicidal speed, intent on beating the pursuing but growing contingent of law enforcement.

Sanderson pulled up on the right side of the Buick waving for it to pull over. The Buick swerved, hitting Sanderson's car on the left side. Sanderson swerved after the collision, nearly losing control. At the same time, the Buick made a sharp left south, along the East River on Roosevelt Drive. Sanderson and the other two pursuing squad cars followed. The Buick took a left on Thirtieth Street.

They were entering downtown Manhattan towards the garment district and traffic was heavier. The Buick wove through cars at times cutting them off. Brakes squealed as they tried to avoid colliding with each other. The Buick ran red lights and relentlessly continued down the four lane thoroughfare. Making an effort to avoid the Buick, cars moving in the intersection collided with each other. Tires screeched and glass shattered in the confusion.

Sanderson swore as he made an effort not to hit the circus of traffic ahead of him. The other NYPD squad cars were doing the same thing. There was no way they were going to catch up.

The Buick ducked down an alley. Sanderson must have missed them in the confusion. He slowed down enough to study the road ahead. They were gone. He couldn't believe it. Sanderson pounded the steering wheel in anger.

Sanderson grabbed the mike of his radio and called dispatch.

"This is Detective Sanderson, put out an all points bulletin on a seventy-five light blue Buick LeSabre in the Manhattan area near West Street. There are two suspects who should be considered armed and dangerous."

CHAPTER THIRTY TWO

Don was still shaking from the confrontation on Long Island. He was anxious and still a little angry but the agitation he felt earlier had subsided. He wondered if Detective Sanderson had caught up with the murderers but he could not concern himself with that now. He needed to get out of New York.

Don began to think about the trip to Wyoming and the long journey ahead. He wanted to see his mother before departing. She always was able to reassure him before he took on a challenge. He was confident of his decision. Actually, he had no choice, but his main intent was to start a new life and he was not sure if his mother would be part of it. Once entering New Jersey from Long Island, he headed south towards Delaware. He was going to visit his mother in Salisbury.

Don drove though New Jersey stopping at the numerous toll booths on the turnpike which nickel-and-dimed him for miles. Finally, he came to the more open spaces along the highway with trees and housing developments. As he traveled though Delaware after getting off I-95, the scenery became rural. The familiar farms and open fields began to appear.

As he drove, he began to think about Marna. She had talked about her childhood in Vineland, an area much like this. He pictured her beautiful face, long, flowing light brown hair, and recalled her lilting laugh as they strolled through Central Park holding each other. He deeply missed her. As the sun shone in his face, Don sighed and wiped away tears forming in his eyes.

Hours later, he crossed into Maryland and arrived at the town of Salisbury. The sun was beginning to set. He drove down Route 13, passed Salisbury State College, entered the residential area and turned onto the familiar street where his mother lived.

He parked the van and took several breaths to relax. He looked in the rear view mirror and straightened his hair. He looked like hell. Oh well, he thought. After what he had been through he was lucky to be in one piece. Mom would notice, but would be glad to see him.

Don walked up to the house and rang the doorbell. Mary was surprised to see him and was quite pleased. Molly greeted him, sniffing Don's pants with her brown nose and rubbing against his legs.

Don told her about leaving work, giving up his apartment and going to Wyoming. Since last year, he had shared with her his interest in doing so. She was supportive and did not question his motives. He showed her the new van which was at this point, standing in the dark with a street light illuminating the vehicle. She suggested that since he was leaving New York, and did not have a permanent residence, he register the van at the DMV with her address and get new tags.

Don spent seven days there. He left at noon on the last day. He hugged her and promised to write.

CHAPTER THIRTY THREE

Although it was not as he had planned, Don at last began his trip to Wyoming. He looked forward to the peace he would find there. The last year and a half were a nightmare beginning with Marna's murder, then the cab accident, his accidental killing of Dan Blackman and his run in with Marna's murderers. He felt gratified that at least, the killers would be brought to justice, hopefully without implicating him.

He sighed and relaxed. The Quaalude withdrawal was over. The agitation had lessoned and his senses more reliable. His feelings of panic had subsided. If only his tolerance of Demerol were reduced, he could begin to feel more in control.

The Lincoln Memorial Highway, also named Route 30 began in New York, was parallel to Route 80, and crossed the entire United States.

He intended to follow it through southern Wyoming connecting to a route taking him north to Jackson. The small town of Jackson, also known as Jackson Hole, is in the northwestern part of the state, next to the Teton Mountains and is just south of Yellowstone. This destination is what Don dreamed about. The exciting western frontier with its beautiful, blue mountains, crystal-clear sky and placid lakes awaited him.

Don traveled east toward Baltimore, took the Chesapeake Bay Bridge and headed north toward Pennsylvania. He then took a westerly route. He crossed Pennsylvania and passed Gettysburg. When approaching Cashtown, he got off the main highway, took local Route 30.

The Cashtown Inn was eight miles east of Gettysburg. It had been there since before the Civil War as a stop for stage coach operators and during the battle of Gettysburg. When approaching Gettysburg, Confederate generals settled there and used it as their headquarters, staying throughout the conflict. The inn was also a hospital for Confederate troops and the basement was used as an operating room. The wounded were brought in by the hundreds during the battle—many of their wounds had cost them their lives. During its history, the inn was known to be haunted. People staying there over the years reported strange occurrences. Don and Kathy had talked about the inn many times but had never visited.

Don passed houses and local businesses on the two lane road when he spotted the inn. It was a barn red color with a white porch and a gray tin roof. Five windows stretched above the porch where a sign was prominently displayed. The porch was low, had a white spoked railing and was almost on the ground with a single step to the front door. Four more windows were spread along the porch where a long swing and rocking chairs rested.

Don carried his bag from the van and checked in with a nice middle-aged woman at a desk in the parlor. He had made reservations at the General A.P. Hill Room. She escorted him up to the second floor and showed him the room on the left.

Now a bed and breakfast, the innkeepers had made an effort to maintain it in period decor and furnishings. A queen size canopy bed was in the center, with draped sheer material across and hanging next to the posts. A quilt comforter with a flowery pattern was made up on the bed. A mahogany night stand stood next to the bed. A mahogany rocking chair, Victorian vanity and bench were on the left by a window. Against the wall between the two front windows was a mahogany table with its leaves down. In the opposite corner was a small settee. White wallpaper with a blue and brownish-yellow striped floral design accented the décor.

Don placed his bag on the settee and sat down to relax. Dinner time was approaching. He washed up in the adjoining bathroom and headed downstairs to the dining room.

After dinner he returned to his room. He was plenty tired from traveling. He had already taken several doses of Demerol throughout the day and took a couple more tablets to remain comfortable. After changing into his pajamas he settled into the bed. He half expected something to happen. This room was the most haunted at the inn. The experience at the Saratt House had peaked his already growing interest in the spirit world.

Morning arrived. Bright sunlight streamed in the windows of the room. As he awoke, he realized that he had slept though the night without even stirring. He must have been totally exhausted. *So much for any paranormal occurrences*, he thought. He didn't hear or see anything.

Don got ready for the day and when going downstairs for breakfast, he left his keys on the night stand. He didn't want to bother with them for the short time he would be eating breakfast.

He had a good meal of scrambled eggs, bacon and toast in the dining room, which was appropriately decorated for the period. He returned to his room and turned the handle of the door. It wouldn't open. He tried again. It was locked! *How could that be?*

After getting the hostess to unlock the door for him, he went over and looked on the night stand. There were the keys as proof that he hadn't absentmindedly locked the door. Don began to think something strange was going on after all.

For the remainder of the day, Don visited Gettysburg. He went to one of the battlefields pivotal to the war and to Don, meant the most—Pickett's Charge. Thousands of Confederate soldiers died in an attempt to overtake the higher ground of the Union. Next to an inscribed granite monument, he stood at the Union side on Cemetery Ridge and looked over the long, flat stretch of ground the Confederate soldiers had to cover to reach the waiting Union forces. He imagined the line of black, large wheeled, artillery stretching for half a mile firing on the advancing ranks of Confederates. He was saddened as he pictured the men and young boys fallen on the blood soaked ground. This dramatic skirmish on the final day marked the finality of the northern defeat of the south at the battle of Gettysburg.

Don returned to the inn, freshened up, and had dinner. He spent some time in the bar next to the dining room having a couple of scotches on the rocks. He returned to his room and prepared to spend his second night there before getting back on the road. Perhaps there would be some additional otherworldly activity.

Don wrote two postcards he bought at Gettysburg—one to Kathy and one to his mother. Pictured were the visitor's center and the three story observation tower. He told them that he was at the inn and that other than getting locked out of his room, nothing had happened thus far.

As the night wore on, Don lay in his bed asleep. He heard a voice.

"Get out," in a whisper.

Don looked at the clock on the night stand it was 2:00 am.

The voice was louder, shouting "Get out."

Startled, Don sat straight up in his bed and looked around. There was no one there. "Could that be my imagination?" He muttered to himself.

Don turned on the lamp on the night stand and looked around the room. Still no one.

He laid back in the bed and pulled the covers up, making an effort to get comfortable. After about an hour of trying, he could not sleep. Feeling the urge to urinate, Don got up and found his way to the bathroom to relieve himself.

When getting back into the bed, he felt someone there! Don jumped out of bed and looked in disbelief at it. In the dark, there was a transparent outline of the top of a man's head sticking out from the covers under which there was, lying on its side, an outline of a human shape. To be sure of what he was seeing, Don stood there for a minute widening his eyes in an effort to adjust his eyesight.

"Who are you?" Don said slowly.

There was no response.

"Are you a Confederate soldier?"

Again, there was no response. The shape remained in the bed.

This was the kind of thing Don had read about. Soldiers who had not passed on to the other side, some thinking they were trapped behind enemy lines, lingered at the inn, not realizing they were dead.

"The Civil War is over," Don stated to his visitor.

The shape disappeared.

Don went over to the night stand and switched on the light. The covers were slightly rumpled but nothing out of the ordinary. He scanned the room and of course, as before, it was empty. He sat on the side of the bed looking around and thinking. He got back into bed and tried to sleep. He lay awake for hours staring into the darkness. Sleep finally arrived as the dim light of dawn approached.

CHAPTER THIRTY FOUR

After leaving Cashtown, Don continued west. As he drove, he couldn't get the strange night he spent there out of his mind. For him, the inn had lived up to its reputation. He couldn't wait to tell Kathy about it.

As the hours wore on, he began to think about his trip to Springfield. It seemed so long ago but the images of the car chase flashed back to him only to give way to the countryside along side the highway. He reflexively checked his rear view mirrors. No sign of anything suspicious. He was lucky that the police had not picked him up outside of New York or traveling through New Jersey. It was curious. Perhaps Detective Sanderson was focused on the suspects related to Marna's murder and the insider trading suspects but not alerted the other jurisdictions. He put a Jackson Browne tape **The Pretender** in the player as he drove. His voice crooned as he played his piano soulfully.

Four days later, after stopping a Pittsburg, he approached Chicago. He stopped at a Holiday Inn motel that he spotted on the outskirts of the city.

After parking the van, Don headed for the office. By this time the sun had already set and the chilly darkness had come. When he got out of the warm vehicle, Don shivered when the chill hit him. The motel clerk was a young woman. She was a pretty brunette who looked the age of a college student working for tuition money. She greeted him cheerfully and checked him in. This time, Don bought four postcards depicting different shots of the Chicago skyscrapers. He paid for the postcards and took his overnight bag out of the van and went to his room.

After getting ready for bed, Don took an extra dose of Demerol. Along with three nightcaps of scotch, these were enough to take the edge off. Since starting the trip, he was maintaining but was beginning to feel jittery and anxious. Without the Demerol, he would not get to sleep.

He sat down at the desk and wrote four cards; one each to his mother, Kathy, Carol and Judith.

Greetings from Chicago! The trip is going great. I plan to spend a few days in Springfield after seeing the sites here. I hope to get to Lincoln by next week. I will keep in touch.

Love,

Donny

CHAPTER THIRTY FIVE

Deputy Rod Jones sat in his office in Rawlins, Wyoming. He sipped his coffee as he tried again to work the crossword puzzle he did daily from the Cheyenne Post. It was a quiet day with little radio traffic. He heard a call on the radio on the desk in the corner.

"This is Patrolman Sizemore calling Carbon County Sheriff, over."

Jones got up out of his chair, walked to the desk and sat down. He put his mouth up to the mike and pressed the bar at its base.

"Deputy Jones here, Patrolman Sizemore. Go ahead."

"I have an abandoned vehicle here on the off ramp from Wagonhound Road near the rest area. The driver is not in sight and appears to have left the vehicle unattended. It looks like the vehicle is from out of state. The van has Maryland tags."

"Is there any sign of anyone near the vehicle?"

"No. Just one set of footprints heading north, away from Elk Mountain."

"Is there any sign of a struggle?"

"No...like I said, it looks like they just wondered off."

Deputy Jones picked up the telephone and dialed a number. "Sheriff, it looks like we have a missing person out on Wagonhound Road exit off eighty," he said in a professional tone. The voice on the other end gave him instructions.

"Okay Sheriff. I will meet you there."

Jones put on his tan uniform jacket with a fake fur collar and a gray triangular patch on each shoulder emblazoned with **Sheriff Carbon County** in bright yellow. In the center of the patch was a light gray and yellow insignia depicting a six-point star. Jones was a short man in his forties, with black hair and a mustache, who appeared as if he had spent too many days on the job seated in a chair. His gut hung over his waistline which was cinched in by a brown belt.

Jones got up, grabbed is black gun belt and strapped it on. It held in its holster a .357 Magnum Colt Python revolver, a black pouch for extra bullets, another for handcuffs and a loop which held a small flashlight.

He took the elevator down from the sheriff's office on the top floor and out the rear entrance of the white marble and brick court house. In the rear parking lot, Jones opened the white door of his dark green cruiser and got in.

CHAPTER THIRTY SIX

Sheriff Robert Coburn drove from his home outside Rawlins to the location reported by his deputy. It was a quiet town. He hadn't had any incidents for some time. Usually there were domestic disturbances when a husband would argue with his wife and she would start throwing dishes at him. Locals of the town sometimes caused trouble at the Fat Boys Bar—mostly alcohol fueled fist fights. At times, people not familiar with the area would get lost and stop at the office for directions.

He wondered what could have happened in this case. Foul play was not very common in Rawlins, but it was a possibility. He knew that whatever the cause, the person could not have gone far.

The sheriff drove along I-80 toward the exit which was fifty miles away. The snow had stopped from earlier in the day. A thin layer of snow lay on the shoulder of the highway and on the surrounding landscape. At least this time it was just a dusting, he thought.

The sheriff was older than his deputy. He had gotten to his position though his many political connections in the town and had been elected ten years ago. Until that time, he had been on the force for five years. At fifty-three years old, he was well built and appeared in good physical shape. His graying light brown hair was long on the sides and greased back.

Coburn parked his cruiser behind the other vehicles on the shoulder of the ramp and put on his baseball cap. Coming to the scene from his home, he was dressed in jeans and a green camouflage hunting jacket. He walked up to Patrolman Sizemore and nodded to Deputy Jones.

"This is the vehicle?" He said to the patrolman examining its exterior. He walked from the rear of the van to the open door, leaning over and studying the interior front seats. He took note of the open cooler, carton of orange juice and the wrappers strewn on the floor. There were no expended shell casings or evidence of blood.

He got in, leaned over the cooler and checked the glove box. He looked through the contents and pulled out a white registration card.

"This vehicle is registered to a Donald Kendall," he said in a low voice, almost to himself.

The sheriff put the registration in the pocket of his jacket. He bent over and looked under the front seat. Other than an empty soda can, there was nothing.

The sheriff then walked back and opened the rear doors. Getting in, he examined the interior of the back of the van, stooping as he went. There was camping gear, a bag of laundry and luggage with men's clothing and personal hygiene items inside. A cardboard box contained canned food and beef jerky.

Coburn got out of the van and scanned the landscape where the footprints led. It was completely devoid of trees or large rocks where someone would be hiding—just those footprints leading to the horizon.

Coburn was a cautious man. He was going to handle this his way. He stood there thinking about the missing man.

"Were going to need some help on this," the Sheriff decided.

"Deputy Jones... call the office on your radio and get three more deputies out here. We may need to use your plane to do an aerial search."

The three officers searched the rest stop. They walked around the surrounding area with a few snow covered picnic tables sitting on concrete roof-covered pavilions. There was no sign of human activity. Elk tracks present in the snow indicated a search for food. The elk had not understood picnicking humans no longer visited.

Officer Jones searched the small rest room building. Apprehensively, he placed his hand on the handle of his gun as he stepped through the door of the men's room. He saw his reflection in the mirror as he walked past the three sinks which stood against the left side of the room. It was empty.

Three stalls stood at the end of the room directly in front of him. He quickly opened the first toilet stall apprehensively looking to the floor for any evidence of a person, lying or perhaps crouching there. He opened the second and third stall. Nothing.

Sizemore checked the women's side of the building with the same result. No one was there.

After the three officers searched the rest stop, another green and white police car arrived with another three deputies. Coburn, Sizemore, and three other deputies spread out fifty feet apart and walked across the open prairie in the direction of the footprints.

The cold wind was blowing. It picked up the snow flakes pushing them in the faces of the searchers. After going five miles north and spending four hours looking, they decided to come back the next day with more men.

CHAPTER THIRTY SEVEN

Detective Sanderson had a suspect in custody directly connected to Marna Anderson's murder. After the confrontation on Long Island, the man wounded by Don Kendall and placed under arrest was picked up at the site. Due to the loss of a large amount of blood, an ambulance was called and he was transported to the emergency room. He was denied bail as a possible flight risk.

Sanderson walked into the interrogation room, closed the door, and sat down. The faded green room was stuffy and had the odor of stale coffee and burnt tobacco.

The man sitting on the other side of the stainless-steel table and smoking a cigarette was identified as Samuel Jenkins. He was a swarthy looking short man with a thick neck, almost absorbing a large head. His muscular arms and chest were evidence that he had spent many hours in the gym. He had a criminal record which included mostly theft and assault. He had spent five years in prison. Jenkins' right shoulder was bandaged and his arm was in a sling.

Sanderson began his questioning.

"Mr. Jenkins you have been advised of your rights…is that correct?"

"Yeah, I have been advised of my rights."

"Mr. Jenkins, we brought you in today for questioning because of your possible involvement in the murder of Marna Anderson." Taking a drag from his cigarette, Jenkins just looked at Sanderson.

"You have already admitted that you worked for Matthew Simms and Augustine."

Jenkins looked annoyed.

"I don't know anybody by the name of Augustine. I worked for Simms. You're getting the wrong idea. I didn't kill anybody."

Sanderson was losing his patience. Jenkins had to be lying.

"That girl is dead and one way or another, you are responsible," he said pounding the table for emphasis.

"You are on parole right now… and our little escapade on Long Island will result in charges of reckless endangerment, resisting arrest and, handgun violations … all of which are a violation of your parole."

"If you cooperate, I could get the State's Attorney to go easy… perhaps drop some of those charges."

Jenkins stared at his questioner and frowned. The wheels were turning. He took several drags from his cigarette and finally said, "Okay… what do you want to know?"

"Were you working for Simms at Stern as part of their security…. right?"

"Yeah…but look, I didn't kill anybody. We were supposed to follow her."

"You mean Marna Anderson?"

"Yeah…and that other guy started seeing her."

"Don Kendall?"

"Yeah… Kendall… but at first we didn't know who he was. After that, we followed them both."

"We wanted to make sure the girl didn't tell anyone about the trades."

"Do you mean the insider trading that is being investigated?"

"Yeah."

"What was her role?"

"I don't know… I guess information she got from her firm. We went to her apartment to scare her. John got a little rough with her and he messed up the room."

"What's John's last name?"

"Weaver."

"Was he the one who drove off in the Crown Vic?"

"Yeah."

"So you and Weaver messed up the room. And maybe you killed her."

"Listen. I'm telling you we didn't. When we left she was alive!"

CHAPTER THIRTY EIGHT

John Weaver was heading west, down I-80. He smiled to himself as he thought about the encounter with the NYPD on Long Island. That was a great piece of driving. He had gotten off the island despite having that flat tire on the front. The police hadn't picked up on the Crown Vic and had pursued the Buick.

After passing Elk Mountain, he had passed Rawlins and was approaching Wamsutter, traveling almost fifty miles. He could not locate the Chevy van on either side of the four lane highway. Weaver cursed at his own stupidity for losing him. Weaver got off the next exit, turned around, and headed east.

After thinking about it, Weaver remembered last seeing the van just before the Arlington exit. The traffic had picked up there. Kendall must have ducked off.

When Weaver approached the Wagonhound exit, he spotted the van pulled over the side of the road. The black an white Highway Patrol car was parked behind it and an officer was looking around.

Weaver kept on driving. He couldn't afford to tangle with any cops.

CHAPTER THIRTY NINE

Deputy Jones drove up to Rawlins Municipal Airport in his police cruiser. He parked the vehicle in a small lot next to the airport's main building, got out and headed for his airplane.

After they had searched the rest area, the sheriff decided to send him to the airport. Jones hoped that a search from the air would be more productive. Already, he had gotten word that the ground search was not bringing results.

The engine sputtered as he fired up his single engine Piper Cub. Jones picked up the mike of radio transmitter and asked for clearance to take off. After a reply emitted from the tiny speaker, Jones pushed the airplane forward. The small plane gained speed down the thin runway and became airborne.

He headed west toward Arlington. Interstate 80 was below him. A few cars and trucks crawled along the four lane highway. There were two lanes each way separated by a wide median area. He passed Elk Mountain which rose to the sky next to him, seeming to reach higher to the heavens as he flew. Below, he spotted the vehicles on the ramp and parked at the rest stop. He studied the ground while changing to a northerly direction towards Route 30. It was mostly open range covered by snow with rocks and patches of dark green pine trees. A farm house or two with barns behind them appeared on the landscape.

He continued to head in a northerly direction for about twenty miles until crossing Route 30 and headed back. He criss-crossed the area several times looking for any sign of a person on foot, which was the only way to get across that prairie. Thinking the worst, he also looked for signs of a body. If there was one, coyotes or magpies circling in hopes of finding food would indicate its presence.

After four hours, the sun was setting and darkness was approaching. Deputy Jones was satisfied that he had scoured the entire area and decided to land.

The next day, Jones and three other officers again searched the area surrounding the Wagonhound exit. This time looking south of Route 80 as well as spreading out over a twenty mile area in each direction. The exhausted men reported finding nothing of value, just a couple of socks, sunflower seeds and a tea pot in an abandoned barn. They weren't even sure if the items belonged to the missing man.

The sheriff called off the search effort. This guy just wasn't in the area any longer.

CHAPTER FORTY

The telephone of Kathy Kendall Wayne rang at her home in Carroll County, Maryland. She was fixing dinner and grabbed the yellow telephone in her kitchen.

It was her mother.

"Kathy," Mrs. Kendall said in a concerned tone.

She hesitated. "Donny's missing."

"Mom, what do you mean missing?"

Normally, Mary Kendall was well spoken and not so vague.

Taken aback, Kathy stopped what she was doing and sat down at the kitchen table. Mary seemed to recover and recounted the details.

"The Wyoming Highway Patrol found his van off an exit off of interstate eighty near a rest area. He must have wondered off and left his van parked on the shoulder with the door open and the engine running. They were able to trace his registration from his van to my Salisbury address. Do you remember when he was moving and added my name and address to the registration here in Maryland?"

"Yeah… I remember. He was in Salisbury after he had given up his apartment."

"Kathy, I am so worried. It doesn't sound like Donny to just wonder off like that."

Kathy sat in disbelief looking out the kitchen window next to the table.

"You're right Mom, this is really bizarre. Something more must have happened than Donny just leaving his van and walking off."

She had gotten several postcards over the last several weeks. They came from Gettysburg, Chicago, Lincoln Nebraska and the last one from Cheyenne Wyoming.

"Have they searched for him," Kathy said, still stunned.

"They have searched for two days on foot and a deputy used his airplane to look. They haven't found much except some footprints."

"They only searched for two days? Mom we need to get out there as soon as possible. These people need to look more than that! Something is wrong."

They decided to fly out to Wyoming together.

Kathy's husband, Bob traveled to Salisbury to pick up his mother-in-law. After arriving back in Woodbine, they would take a flight from Baltimore-Washington International Airport.

It was dusk when Bob Wayne arrived in Salisbury. He drove down the small residential street where Mary Kendall lived. Bob was well acquainted with Salisbury. He had made frequent trips during his relationship with Kathy over the last fifteen years. His brown eyes concentrated on the road as he drove. His hair and eyebrows were a burnt red color and his weathered complexion revealed many hours spent on his boat.

Returning to the western shore enroute to Woodbine, they traveled in the tan Chevette on Route 50 towards the Chesapeake Bay Bridge. The eastern shore roads were rural. When driving on the two lane highway it was not unusual to see a farm tractor pulling a piece of equipment in the left lane. They passed vacant roadside stands which sold locally grown fruit and vegetables. Empty fields with farms, woods and an occasional house appeared in the car windows as the darkness descended upon them.

Mary thought about her missing son as the Chevette traveled down the highway at sixty miles an hour. She still couldn't believe that the bizarre circumstances of his disappearance. He had always been good at everything he did—very competent. He would never lose his bearings and wander on the prairie unless there were some very strange circumstances.

Soon they were outside Cambridge.

Suddenly, a deer appeared in the headlight beams. It jumped in the path of the car. Bob tried to avoid the collision but it was too late. He hit the brakes as the Chevette plowed into the full-grown deer and careened off the road into a drainage ditch. The impact sent Mary flying. Bob was more alert and was able to brace himself with the steering wheel. The grill and hood crumbled under the impact as the car was jolted to a halt.

Woozy, Bob stared in disbelief at the now disabled car. Steam rose from the hood. The radiator was crushed. The hood was folded up like a bent playing card. He checked himself to see if there were any lacerations in his upper body. His legs felt alright. He turned to Mary.

"Are you alright?" Mrs. Kendall looked shaken up.

"I hit my right side," she said, wincing in pain and holding her arm.

"We need to call an ambulance."

"No, no, we really need to get to Wyoming."

"Are you sure?" Bob was concerned. She looked as if she may have needed medical attention.

"Yes," Mary said emphatically. "Lets find a way to get out of here."

Bob retrieved a flash light, got out of the Chevette and inspected the front end. As he suspected, it was not repairable. The grille was completely smashed in and the radiator was leaking copious amounts of green antifreeze in the ditch mixing with the runoff water already there. The front fender was severely bent and was pressed against the left front tire. Bob shone the flashlight down the shoulder of the road. The deer lay across the ditch. It was a large male with a not fully formed set of horns protruding from its head, blood running from its mouth and eyes.

Bob had to get to a phone. He walked around surveying the surrounding area with his flashlight. To the right were the other two west-bound lanes which were totally devoid of traffic. Beyond were some empty fields where crops had been harvested.

He walked down the shoulder of the road on the side of the wrecked car. After a few hundred feet he spotted a small house. The glow of lights on the first floor indicated its presence. Reluctant to bother the occupants, he walked up the small sidewalk. The house was in disrepair and Bob thought that it must have been there for seventy-five years. It was two stories with a small porch supported by two thin, round stanchions. As he approached he noticed the paint peeling off the wood of the porch and door frame.

Bob knocked loudly on the screen door hanging loosely on its hinges. A few minutes passed. A black face appeared in the window peering out beyond a pulled back white curtain. It disappeared. Slowly, the front door opened. An old woman appeared peeking out of the cracked door. Her gray hair was tied back in a bun framing her dark face and wide brown eyes.

"What do you want?" Her scratchy voice inquired.

"Maam, can I please use your telephone. I hit a deer back there and my mother-in-law is hurt." Bob knew that Mary was going to refuse treatment but he wanted to portray a sense of urgency.

The woman's stern demeanor changed once learning of the circumstances.

"Sure…the telephone is there in the living room."

Bob went in, picked up the receiver of an ancient telephone on an end table. The rotary telephone clicked as he dialed Kathy's number. Kathy's phone rang three times.

"Hello," Bob was glad to hear Kathy's voice.

"Kathy," Bob said trying to remain calm.

"You wouldn't believe what just happened… I hit a deer and wrecked the car."

"Oh no! Are you alright?"

"I'm okay but your mother seems to be hurt.

"She's hurt? How bad?"

"She hit her arm and maybe her hip on the passenger's side door."

"She needs to go to the hospital to get checked out."

"I thought so too, but she insists on getting back to your house so that you can catch your flight."

"That sounds like Mom," Kathy said with a little humor.

"Where are you now?"

"I'm calling from a house close to where we hit the deer," Bob said, looking at the old woman, now grinning, showing a missing incisor.

"It's dark now. We're going to find a motel. In the morning we can take care of the car. I don't think I can drive it."

"Okay… Call me when you get there. Bye, I love you."

"Bye, Bob said." Kathy hung up.

Bob thanked the woman and asked her about the closest motel. There was one a half mile down the road. He returned to the wrecked car and told Mary of his plan to stay the night. He helped her out of the car. She appeared able to walk and any injuries she had were not serious.

After walking down the dark road for what seemed like hours, a sign, **Holly's Motel** glowing in green and red, appeared in the distance to the weary travelers. Little green and red holly leaves blinked on and off in the corners of the sign.

Relieved, Bob checked them in and made sure that Mary was comfortable in the room. They would have to wait till morning to have the Chevette towed and get a rental car. Then they would complete the trip home.

CHAPTER FORTY ONE

Kathy and Mary Kendall departed on their flight enroute to Wyoming. They would have to make a connection in Denver to fly to the municipal airport there. Thankfully, Mary had not sustained any major injuries in the accident. She had bruising to her right hip and arm. A determined woman, she was not going to be stuck in any emergency room while her son was missing.

It was snowing in Denver when they landed. The storm was affecting the entire central section of the country and was likely to have hit Wyoming as well.

They boarded a smaller, commuter plane. It was a nineteen-fifties type twin prop plane which held twenty passengers. The space was small with two seats crammed on each side of the isle. Kathy sat next to the small, rectangular window.

She couldn't help but think about an episode of the Twilight Zone. In the show, William Shatner looks out and sees a creature on the wing—dismantling it. He excitedly tells the stewardess. She looks out the window and there is no creature. She tells him not to worry and to calm down. The creature comes back and continues his work tearing at the prop engine. He again tries to report it and no one believes him. He continues to look out the window observing the hairy, deranged creature. The bizarre experience drives him beyond sanity. After they land, he is removed from the plane by men in white coats, kicking and screaming on a stretcher.

They finally approached the border of Wyoming and the captain made an announcement over the intercom.

"Due to poor weather conditions, we will be landing in Cheyenne. As we approach, please fasten your seat belts."

They descended towards the airport. Scaring all aboard, the plane bounced a few times. Kathy pictured the fragile plane spinning out of control in a suicidal dive. Kathy and Mary held hands and their breaths as the plane finally set down on the runway.

After the small plane landed, Kathy and Mary learned that they would be provided a bus to travel to their destination.

They boarded the Greyhound bus along with the other people intending to go points east. The snow was falling at a steady rate. The flakes were large and stuck to items of clothing worn by the passengers. The two women found a seat next to each other resigned to the fact that their trip was further delayed. They would have to travel one hundred twenty-five miles to Rawlins, where the Carbon County Sheriff's office was located.

As the snow continued to fall, the bus traveled along the mountainous terrain of the interstate at a rapid pace and was making good time. They made one stop at Laramie, discharged some passengers and continued on to their destination. At last, they arrived in Rawlins. Having reservations, they checked in at the Holiday Inn.

The next day, the two women took a cab to the sheriff's office. They approached the courthouse which housed the Carbon County Sheriff's Department. A layer of white snow covered the front lawn.

The small courthouse was a three story building with a white brick exterior and marble steps placed before a marble-trimmed glass entrance. Large lantern-like fixtures hung on each side. To the left, Kathy noticed an American flag which flew on a tall, white flagpole. The two women entered the court house and after inquiring at the desk in the lobby, they took the elevator up to Sheriff Coburn's office on the third floor.

They walked into the office. There was a counter with a swinging door at the end for access to two officer's desks beyond. As they approached the counter, an officer got up from his desk to greet the visitors.

"Hello, I'm Deputy Jones." The officer smiled, sizing up the strangers. The two women were obviously related. The younger of the two was dressed in slacks, a fashionable light brown winter coat with a fur collar. Her shoulder length blond hair was held back with barrettes off her face and rested on her coat collar. The older woman, wearing a light blue winter coat, its collar upturned, and glasses framing her short, blond-highlighted hair, her brow furrowed, appeared angry. Both attractive, their blue eyes anxiously gazed at him. Mrs. Kendall, trying to be diplomatic, spoke.

"Hello Deputy Jones, we are here to speak to Sheriff Coburn. I am Mrs. Kendall, Donald Kendall's mother. This is my daughter Kathy. We came out here to talk to you about his disappearance. The sheriff notified us that he is missing."

"Oh yes… we were expecting you two yesterday."

"We were delayed because of the storm," Mrs. Kendall reported.

"Now that you are here… I will get the sheriff."

Jones left the front counter and walked back to the rear of the room and knocked on the office door. Sheriff Coburn came out of the office and greeted the women.

"Good morning, ladies," he said, smiling broadly. The sheriff was now wearing his uniform, his firearm absent. His light brown shirt and dark brown pants looked official but there was an informal air about him.

"I heard you little ladies were coming… but I don't think there is anything much we can do for you." The sheriff held the swinging counter door and motioned for the women to proceed to his office. They walked though the door marked **Sheriff** on the translucent glass.

The office was mostly empty; devoid of pictures on the walls or other personalized items. Just a desk, file cabinet and book case which looked like it was a catch-all for road maps, Field and Stream magazines, memos, bulletins and opened Manila envelopes. Coburn showed them chairs placed in front of the desk. Still anxious, Mrs. Kendall leaned forward in her chair.

"Sheriff, we are here to look into my son's disappearance. Do you have any new leads?" Coburn looked at her impatiently.

"I know you came all this way to try and move things along… but believe me we have done all that we can to find him. He is no longer in this area. Sorry."

"Sheriff, we heard about your so-called search. We think that you need to do more," Mary said, looking at Kathy.

"Deputy Jones out there knows every fence, sage brush and rock on that prairie," Coburn emphasized, pointing to the outer office.

"He believes that your son is somewhere else… perhaps in another county."

"Why can't we bring in some help," Kathy said, pleading.

"There must be other resources…do you have a Civil Air Patrol in this area?"

The sheriff was becoming annoyed. "Look little girl …we have done a thorough search and I see no need to bring in all kinds of people from the outside wandering around in my county. It would be chaos."

Kathy frowned and looked at Coburn who was obviously referring to her youth. She didn't appreciate his attitude and decided not to comment on the reference.

"Sheriff my son is missing… I can't believe that you won't do any more to look for him!" Mrs. Kendall said angrily.

"What else have you done to investigate? Did you go over his van and the surrounding area to look for evidence?"

"I took a look in his van for any obvious evidence. Other than the strange way the van was left, there was nothing out of the ordinary."

Kathy paused, not believing what she heard.

"What about fingerprints or footprint impressions…any kind of evidence."

"Little girl, we did not collect any evidence of that kind because at this point, it is a missing person's case, not anything else."

"Where is his van now?"

"We pulled it off the exit ramp and into the parking lot of the rest area. I'm sorry …. we have done all that we can."

Mary and Kathy just looked at each other in disgust. They weren't going to just let this go. This sheriff wasn't going to pursue it any further. He was overconfident and condescending. The only other option left was for them to act on their own.

CHAPTER FORTY TWO

Matt Daniels had grown up in Casper, Wyoming. It was a small town with only one hundred thirty residents north of the Pathfinder Reservoir next to the North Platte River. He had a good life here. At age thirty and divorced, he had done pretty well for himself. Although he had to rent the small property it sat on, he owned a trailer. He liked to think of it as a "mobile home." The place had a living room/dining area populated by a worn sofa, a black vinyl reclining chair and a small dining room table with dangling leafs. There was a nice bathroom and in the back portion of his "mobile home" were two bedrooms.

Matt had a good job as a rig operator for the Midwestern Oil Drilling Company. Standing at five feet eleven inches, he had deep set blue eyes and long, light brown hair combed back with a wave in front. He was pleased with the bushy brown mustache he had recently grown. By most, he was considered a pretty good looking guy. He had some luck with women here and there and even got married once. It didn't last. He was impatient, abrupt and didn't handle things well. Maybe marriage just wasn't for him.

He had a few scrapes with the law years back. When he was laid off, he was dealing drugs for a time. Nothing hard, just marijuana, to make ends meet. He got mixed up with some bad people. It all closed in on him. He was arrested and charged with sale and distribution. In exchange for providing information about the distribution network, his sentence was reduced to five years.

It was a Tuesday morning. He had a job in Medicine Bow. It was going to be a long drive. Holding his coffee mug, Matt walked down the steps of the white and green trailer. He got in his black Ford pickup truck, started it up, pulled out of the gravel driveway and drove toward Route 220.

CHAPTER FORTY THREE

Kathy and Mary decided to take the drive out to the exit on I-80 to look at Don's van and to the surrounding area for themselves. Kathy drove the sub-compact rental car east from Rawlins. They traveled the hilly highway for sixty miles spotted the Wagonhound exit, and pulled off.

As they drove down the exit ramp Don's gray Chevy van came into view. It was parked on the lot to the side of the rest stop. Beyond it, the flat, barren landscape seemed to mock them in their desperation to find their loved one.

The women parked behind the van. They got out of the car and approached it, peering in the windows. The interior of the van looked to be disheveled as if someone had been rummaging through it. Don was much neater. He wouldn't have left it that way.

When Kathy came up to the driver's side she saw the door keyhole was jimmied. The medal was twisted and bent. Kathy looked at it in disbelief. The police had not said anything about the van being broken into. She looked across the roof at her mother.

"Mom, this van has been broken into."

She opened the door and sat inside. The red and white cooler sat on the passenger's side seat. Mary opened the passenger's side which was not locked, and looked into the front of the van. The glove box was open; a pair of sunglasses, an owner's manual and a small manufacturer's touch up paint container lay on the floor below.

"Kathy, it looks like someone went though the glove compartment. There is no way to tell if anything was taken. Didn't you tell me that the sheriff's department found the registration?"

"Yeah Mom… they told me that on the telephone. That's how they were able to find us."

Kathy spotted something under her foot, raised her right leg, and looked behind it. A credit card receipt. She picked it up and examined the yellow paper. It was dated November twenty-first and the amount was four dollars. To spend such a small amount, he must have stopped at a convenience store in the last two days. She looked at the stamped section to learn where his credit card was used. The ink was smudged and Kathy could not make out the name.

"What about Don's address book?"

Mrs. Kendall moved the cooler to the back seat and got in the van for a closer look. They both looked over the area around the two front seats. Kathy crawled in back and continued to look though a variety of items on the floor and a few boxes. The address book was not there. The other items looked as if he had left them behind in a hurry.

They looked for themselves around the rest area. They spotted two elk in the distance walking toward the horizon. Otherwise, the place was empty.

CHAPTER FORTY FOUR

The next day, after returning to Rawlins, the women decided to split up and canvas the places where Don would likely to have gone. Mary rented a separate car in Rawlins. She planned to stop at local convenience stores to ask employees and patrons if they had seen him.

Kathy inquired about the location of the Lincoln Memorial near a place called Sherman Hill, ten miles southeast of Laramie. She learned that the monument was erected on the Lincoln Highway, which preceded the building of interstate 80 to improve travel from east to west though Nebraska. She decided that this was a place Don would certainly stop. Perhaps a clue would reveal what had happened to him.

She traveled on Route 80, back towards the Cheyenne airport they had landed at two days earlier. Sherman Hill would not be hard to find. It was the highest point on I-80 at the edge of a rest area. She had to travel one hundred miles to reach it. The landscape looked familiar. She crossed the Medicine Bow Mountains, the highest of which stretched to the south. She could see the valleys below populated with grasslands, rocks and stands of pine trees.

Kathy smiled and laughed out loud when remembering her experiences with Donny. She thought about driving toward Frederick, Maryland looking forward to spending time with Don at the Monocacy National Battlefield hunting for artifacts. This was a prime spot for hunting because Confederate and Union forces had engaged in battle on the banks of the Monocacy River. Confederate forces camped there before marching towards Washington D.C. with the intention of invading the city.

They had been on many trips previously. At the battlefields in Gettysburg they looked for anything worth finding. Without a metal detector, Don had a knack for locating a spots to probe the soil. He studied the Matthew Brady photographs of the battlefields to locate the exact spots where troops had fought and died. They usually found something—tent pegs, musket balls, bayonets and even a union soldier's belt buckle.

Kathy remembered driving into the Monocacy State Park entrance, and spotting Don's green Sentra in the parking lot. Don got out of his car slowly—today he looked like he was feeling some pain. He had on a soft down coat which covered his upper body. The light brown coat was lighter and softer which spared his neck and back.

"Kathy!" he said enthusiastically as he walked toward her and gave her a hug. He hadn't seen her since she cared for him at his apartment after the accident.

"Well, I guess it's time to look for some more Civil War artifacts for our collection."

Since his recovery, he was dying to get out again and look. Don got the metal detector of out his trunk. It was one of those with a handle, long, broom-like extension with a small metal disc on the end.

"I know of a perfect place to look," Don said enthusiastically.

They walked a couple hundred yards to the edge of the river until reaching a place where the river had sculpted out a steep grade.

"Kathy, this is the spot."

"Donny, that is pretty far down," Kathy said with trepidation.

"I know. I don't think you will have much trouble."

"You want me to go down there?" Kathy said, as she looked at him skeptically.

"Kathy, you know I can't do it with my back."

Kathy reluctantly agreed.

After finding a place to crawl down to the riverside, Kathy stood on the muddy bank. Debris was scattered around the area, washed up from the previously swollen river. Don stood above looking down.

Don yelled to Kathy, "Look under that log."

Holding the metal detector in one hand and probing with the other—she was not into this. She squeamishly moved the log, half expecting a snake's head to appear and bite her. Kathy scanned around it with the detector.

Yelling again, "How about that rock there."

Cursing under her breath and half expecting some unforeseen slimy creature or insect to appear, she flipped over a large, flat rock with both hands and probed with the detector.

After looking for two hours, Kathy had found two tent pegs and two Union uniform buttons.

Smiling, she remembered that she was grateful that she wasn't bitten once.

CHAPTER FORTY FIVE

As the interstate rose to a higher elevation, Kathy approached Sherman Hill.

On the right, the monument came into view. A monolith of stone with a large carved head of Abraham Lincoln appeared on the horizon. The **Summit Rest Area** sign pointed to its location.

Kathy got off the exit and parked in the lot next to the monument. It was more of a sculpture than a statue. It was certainly different than any monument she had seen. Reddish-brown sculpted rectangular shapes formed a thirty foot structure with Abe's lifelike head at the top, gazing in the distance. A black and bronze plaque was mounted at the bottom. Kathy slowly walked up six steps and stood on a snow covered platform surrounded by railings.

Kathy took in the pristine view of the serene setting. Her mind re-focused on her reason for coming there — to look for Don. She walked down the steps off the platform and around the wall on each side of the main part of the sculpture. She wasn't sure exactly what she was looking for, just any evidence Donny may have left.

She scoured the grounds and found her way over to a vacant rest area building with an American flag flying next to it.

She approached the door of the visitor's center and knocked, just in case a park employee was inside. There was no response. Kathy looked in a window to the left of the door, trying to get a glimpse of something though the partially broken Venetian blind which was lowered behind it. The place was empty—perhaps for the winter season.

Curious, Kathy looked around and behind the building. Three metal barrels sat there, perhaps used for trash. She looked inside each one... for something... a body?

After looking for a half an hour, Kathy was sure that if her brother had been here, there was no evidence of it.

Mary drove her white Pontiac rental car west from Rawlins to the nearby town of Elk Mountain to discover who had possibly seen her son. She entered the small town off of the I-80 exit and just outside the town limits. Commanding her attention, the mountain stood in the distance beyond the flat prairie. It had a gradual slope which led to the face which was straight up. It was a beautiful sight extending across the horizon, greenish-blue with white snow on its summit.

She noticed a small convenience store off to the right. Still thinking about the receipt Kathy had found in the van, perhaps Donny had stopped off the interstate to buy something there.

She pulled into the gravel driveway. The small store stood by itself. A sign in white letters advertising **Robertson's** hung from the porch ceiling. She got out of the car buttoning up her light blue coat. She walked up to the small porch. It had just one step and supporting posts on each corner. Wooden chairs and a rusty old fashioned stove populated it. She approached the front door which had a glass window divided in four sections. There was an **OPEN** sign in the lower corner.

As Mary walked in, a bell attached to the door frame announced her arrival. The store had small isles of grocery items to the right. Against the wall was an old Coca Cola machine. A counter stood to the left. Shelves below it stocked candy. A frozen ice cream case sat next to the counter.

A young woman who looked like she was in her mid-twenties walked to the front of the store as Mary walked in.

"Hello," Mary said to the woman.

"Hello, may I help you?" The woman smiled warmly. Her freckled face and blue eyes had a welcoming quality.

"I'm looking for my son who passed though this area and may have been here." Mary held up the 3x 4 snap shot of Don to show the young woman. The she took it and examined it for several seconds trying to place the man in the photograph.

"No… I'm sorry. I don't recall seeing him.

"Are you sure? It probably wasn't that long ago that he was in this area. He may have charged some items he bought."

She took out the credit card receipt and showed it to the woman. Mrs. Kendall looked pleadingly at her.

"He is missing."

"Maam… I am sorry, but I have not seen him. Besides, we don't take credit cards."

"Thank you," Mary said cordially. She was beginning to understand that this was going to be no easy task.

Mary left the store and drove further into town.

CHAPTER FORTY SIX

Kathy continued to look for signs of her brother. She traveled east on I-80 in the direction of Cheyenne looking for any possible place he may have gone or have been taken. She noticed a structure on a side road, perhaps a collapsed shed. She took the next exit off the interstate and headed back down a two lane local road. Spotting the structure to the left about two hundred yards down, she made a turn and headed towards it. The snow on the flat land around the structure was disturbed and several sets of footprints led into it.

Kathy pulled over to the side of the road and jumped out of the car. If there was anyone walking around, it was apparent that they weren't in the area. Half running, she excitedly approached the structure to see what was inside. The small wooden building had toppled over. The roof lay on one side and with the sides propped up it formed a triangle. She crouched down trying to see in the darkness. As she went in, a small stream of light flowed in what must have been a side window. It was enough to light the back of she shed to see anything inside. Crouching, she moved forward.

"Donny, are you there?" Nothing.

Suddenly, a startled blackbird flew out, wings fluttering; it hit a piece of wood, and made a loud thud. Startled, Kathy jumped back and screamed.

Fear that something terrible has happened to her brother over took her. She sat down on the cold ground and began to cry. "My god Donny…where are you?" She said out loud.

She quickly composed herself and wiped her eyes with her hand. She had to be strong.

Kathy got back in the car and drove back on I-80 towards Cheyenne. She recalled a museum that Don had mentioned on the last postcard she had received.

CHAPTER FORTY SEVEN

Mrs. Kendall headed further into Elk Mountain to question anyone who may have seen her son. She stopped at the only other place in the tiny town accessible to the public—the Elk Mountain Hotel.

She approached the two story structure. In disrepair, it looked as if it was built during Victorian times. The front had a double porch with four white posts and a green railing running the entire length of each. An ornate, green trimmed pointed roof with a small window in the center topped the structure.

Mary entered the large doorway at the front. She approached the check-in desk. An elderly desk clerk studied her as she walked across the empty lobby with the photo of Don in her hand.

She introduced herself to the clerk and got right to the point.

"I am looking for my son who has been missing. I have a photograph here."

She held it up to show it to him.

"Sir, have you seen him? Perhaps he stayed at or stopped by this hotel."

The gray-haired man took the photograph in his wrinkled fingers and held it up close to his face training his bifocal glasses on it. He paused, forming a mental picture. Apprehensive, Mary held her breath for a second hoping the old man would remember. At last he spoke.

"I'm sorry... I haven't seen this fella'."

"Are you sure?"

"I wish for your sake I had...but I'm afraid not. You ought to try the bar through there." The old man pointed toward the back part of the building. Mary walked down a hallway and found a separate section of the hotel. She walked into a dark, smoky room with a long bar to the right and stools with two customers perched on them. Country music blared from the jukebox. Waylon Jennings was singing one of his better known tunes. Tables with a few patrons sitting in chairs, western hats tilted back, engaged in conversation, were scattered throughout the room.

Mary walked up to the bar and showed the picture to the bartender and the men on the stools. She did the same for the others in the place. They shook their heads to the negative. This place began to depress Mary and she was glad to leave.

Undaunted, Mary got back on I-80 and drove back towards Rawlins. She got of the interstate and traveled in a northerly direction on Route 30. She stopped at more local mom-and-pop shops showing the picture. She inquired at a store called Snyder's in Hanna and continued on Route 30 for forty-five miles to Rock River stopping at Greenwood's Grocery.

When leaving Rock River, she noticed a bar there. A small neon sign in the picture window simply stated **Bar and Grille**. The place had no more than five people sitting on round stools at a bar counter fifteen feet long. No one had a clue about seeing Don.

After leaving, she spotted a small house across the street with a sign in the window which read, **Psychic.**

At this point she was desperate. None of her travels that day had given her any hope of finding her son. She had no experience with the occult and had never gone to a psychic. Like most people, she was skeptical. Kathy had told her about the medium that Donny had hired to contact Mary Saratt. The woman seemed to have some success.

Although she hoped her son was still alive, the possibility that he was dead still existed. But really, a psychic? Her children believed that looking beyond the present reality was possible.

She opened the door and found herself walking into a small living room. A table with several chairs was placed in the middle. A woman came through a curtain from the back of the house. Mary expected to see someone looking like a gypsy with black eye makeup and tons of dangling jewelry. The woman looked as if she could have been a hippie from California who had settled east of the Rockies. She was wearing a worn pair of jeans and a long, flowing cotton blouse; open in the front, adorned with red embroidered flowers. She appeared a little older than Donny.

"Hello," the woman said extending her hand to Mary.

"My name is Sister Angelina." The woman smiled at Mary as she spoke. Her countenance was subdued. Naturally pretty, she was wearing no makeup. Her curly, brown hair was pulled back on her forehead, revealing a faded, red wine stain birthmark.

Her apprehension subsiding, Mary extended her hand to grasp the young woman's.

"Why do you wish to see me today?"

"I am looking for my son. He has disappeared."

The woman motioned for Mary to sit down at the table. They sat facing each other. A crystal ball sat in the center of the table between them.

"Do you have any object which he owned or may have given you?" Mary thought for a moment. Her hand felt the necklace she was wearing.

"My son gave me this." She took off the gold chain with a pendant and gave it to her. Gazing into the crystal ball and bending her head slightly downward, the psychic felt the necklace. Mary looked at her intently, anticipating a response.

"I see a young man." The woman paused—trying to form a picture in her mind.

"He has light brown hair and blue eyes... he is lost...sick... but he is alive."

CHAPTER FORTY EIGHT

Kathy approached the exit off I-80 towards Cheyenne. She was looking for the place which Don had mentioned in the postcard—Wyoming State Museum. She took the Route 87 exit onto Route 30, West Lincoln Highway. She saw a sign which directed her toward the museum on Central Avenue.

She parked the car and approached the one story white building. She pushed open one side of a double door and entered the front of the museum.

The place was empty. It appeared she was the only visitor. An unattended glass display case with a counter stood to the right. Directly ahead was a diorama of a landscape with rocks, prairie and mountains in the distance with **The Wild Bunch** labeled on the side. She imagined it to be some kind of display about the local wild life.

Not seeing anyone in the area, she continued to walk though the museum looking at the exhibits. A buffalo head hung above her with a sign, **The Bison-Monarch of the Plains.** Continuing through the museum, a sheep wagon display stood in the corner. The square green base with wagon wheels looked similar to a covered wagon with doors in the back. A stuffed sheep stood in front of it looking as if it were grazing. As Kathy walked past a rectangular Lincoln Highway marker box with a basrelief face of Abe and an **L** painted on it, she spotted someone. Kathy approached a matronly looking woman who was walking back in the direction of the curio display case.

"Excuse me. I was hoping that you could help me."

The woman looked at Kathy. A smile appeared on her face, lined from many hours outdoors.

"What can I do for you dear?"

"My bother has disappeared and I am looking for him. I think he stopped by here on the way to Jackson."

She took out the photo she had of Don standing next to a cannon from their trip to Springfield. The woman's hazel eyes widened with recognition.

"Why yes… he was here I think… a couple of weeks ago."

"He was?" Kathy said hopefully.

"Well… I think this fella' looks like him. The fella' left in a hurry. His brief case was still there next to the diorama."

"Do you still have it?"

"Sure… it's behind the counter over there."

The woman went behind the display case and handed her the brown Samsonite briefcase with a brown plastic handle. Kathy looked at it in disbelief. Her brother would never leave something that important. He wasn't absentminded. Something distracted him.

CHAPTER FORTY NINE

The SEC investigation was beginning to bring results. Sanderson was getting information which would provide evidence to link Simms, and perhaps Augustine to Marna Anderson's murder.

Anderson had worked for the Wall Street firm of Wilson Jones. Though her position as a broker, she had obtained information from bank executives and pension fund managers who dealt with her firm. Management decisions about mergers which her firm handled and information about the acquisition of new mutual funds under their control were made available to Matthew Simms and Ralph Augustine of Stern Investment Group.

Dan Blackman had been the go-between. After he was called by Anderson, he would call Simms and Augustine with the information. After being threatened, and worried he would be implicated in the murder, he went to the SEC authorities and made a deal. He would be immune from prosecution if he fully cooperates.

Wiretaps were ordered. The information helped investigators indentify the participants and the firms involved. Anderson was being followed by security employees of Stern Investment Group who were ordered to report back. Don Kendall, Marna Anderson's boyfriend, was also followed and harassed. The impression was that Anderson had revealed the scheme to him and would tell authorities.

Sanderson looked at the case file. The coroner's report stated that the cause of Anderson's death was asphyxia due to strangulation. Fingerprints at the scene belonged to two suspects who worked for Simms; John Weaver and Samuel Jenkins. Prints belonging to Don Kendall, who discovered the body at the apartment, were also found. Crime scene investigators found another set of prints which, at this time could not be identified. Also found was an object not belonging to the victim—a watch.

CHAPTER FIFTY

D on, Don... you are close to the truth, Mary Saratt's voice said faintly, as Don slowly awoke face down with hay in his mouth.

Mary Saratt stood there in front of him dressed as he had remembered her at his apartment. She wore a blue dress, white blouse, a red scarf tied under its white collar, fastened with a broach at the neck—her brown hair parted in the middle and pulled back in a bun, looking like a Civil War photo—only glowing and in color. She was smiling now, holding her hand out beckoning him toward her. Then she was gone.

He shivered uncontrollably, wrapping his arms around him, holding his down coat for warmth. He became aware of the fowl smell of vomit. He looked down at the front of his coat. It stained the brown fabric. He felt the dampness of his sweat drenched shirt. Subsiding now, he remembered the waves of pain cramping his stomach and legs.

He looked around to assess where he was. Sunlight shone through warped boards making a striped pattern on the straw covered dirt floor in front of him.

Still feeling groggy, he lifted his upper body on his elbows and looked around. He was in the corner of a barn. It didn't appear that anyone had used it for some time. Part of the roof was collapsed and mourning doves co-cooed in the snow covered loft above. Looking at the straw covered floor in front of him, the forty-five lay there. A foggy memory of being afraid and fleeing the van came momentarily, and was lost. The voices of people talking and the buzzing of a plane overhead drifted through his confused brain. How long ago was it? Was it five days ago or yesterday?

As the day progressed, he began to feel better. His stomach cramps had subsided and the nausea had passed. His hands were still shaking.

Why was I so sick? After reflection, it became clear. His body had become used to the Demerol for pain and his drinking probably didn't help. Now that he was out of medication, the resulting effects were taking their toll. Don sat up. He winced as the pain coursed through his body.

There was a knapsack on the floor. He found a plastic quart container of water which lay next to it. He began to remember drinking out of it to quench his thirst as waves of nausea passed through him. Gripping it in his trembling hands he took several large gulps. Not remembering what was in it, he looked in the knapsack. There was an empty prescription bottle, a map and two packs of beef jerky. Ravenous with hunger, he took out a pack of beef jerky and tore the plastic with his teeth. He took several bites and choked it down.

Feeling more comfortable and aware, Don began to assess the situation. He had been there long enough to overcome the sickness he felt from withdrawing. His back hurt but he would have to deal with it. The Demerol was gone. He would have given all of his worldly possessions for tall glass of scotch on the rocks.

Feeling unsteady, he got to his feet. He walked over to the barn entrance. An abandoned farmhouse was a few hundred feet away. Beyond it, the snow covered prairie stretched out for miles.

With his knapsack on his shoulder, Don slowly walked to the old farmhouse. It was a two story structure with peeling paint and large, dirty, curtainless windows. As he approached, the back porch came into view. It was obvious that no one had lived there for some time. A rusty screen door hung from one hinge, long forgotten. Perhaps the occupants had left behind some items useful to him. Don stepped on the porch, pulled off the screen door and tossed it to the side. Peering inside the rectangular windows, he tried the rusty door handle. It creaked and with a push, opened. He entered the kitchen. Looking around, he stepped into the empty room.

On the far side, cabinets stood over the sink, perhaps a pantry. Investigating its contents, he found two cans of baked beans; one can of Spam and a can of creamed corn sitting on the shelf. He took the items and but them in his knapsack. He rummaged through the drawers next to the sink, and found a can opener. So far, this was what he needed.

He investigated the rest of the house. There were just empty rooms with pieces of discarded, broken furniture littering them. He went back to the kitchen and took the map out of the knapsack. He dusted off a kitchen chair and sat down. He studied it for several minutes and decided that he must be somewhere between the Wagonhound exit off of I-80 and Medicine Bow to the north.

How did he get here? Don began to remember.

CHAPTER FIFTY ONE

Don was standing at the Lincoln Monument after parking his van. It was a very quiet place. On the platform at the base of the tall sculpture, he spotted a Crown Victoria parked in the rear of the rest stop. It was exactly like *the* Crown Vic he had encountered many times before. Not sure it was the same car, he paused to get a better look. It was Weaver. How did he get there?

Don instinctively felt fear. There had been too many close calls in the past and he wondered if the others were nearby.

He bounded down the steps two at a time, adrenalin running though his body. Breathing heavily, he ran to his van and jumped in. He turned the key. It tried to start but stalled. The Crown Vic was at the other end of the parking lot, slowly driving through looking for the van. Don cranked the Chevy again. The engine sprang to life. He backed out of the space and jammed it in drive. He sped out of the lot down the exit ramp. Getting on I-80 he drove the van at a suicidal speed. Recognizing his vehicle, the Crown Vic quickly followed him.

Don tore down I-80 for what seemed like an eternity trying to lose the Crown Vic. Although he didn't spot any additional cars following him, he thought there could be others. He saw some exits come up. First was Elk Mountain, then Arlington…the Crown Vic was gaining on him. Traffic was beginning to pick up and he saw his opportunity. An exit marked **Arlington** appeared on the road. He ducked onto the exit.

After coming off the ramp, a restaurant was on the right. Quickly, he drove into the small parking lot. Noticing a driveway to the rear, he pulled down it and parked.

Anxiously looking for the Crown Vic, he quickly walked and entered the front door. There was a counter and booths inside. Going to a corner in the back, and taking a booth, he sat down facing the door. The waitress saw him come in and took his order. She brought a cup of coffee to the booth, placing it on the table. Sipping his coffee he waited and watched. One or two customers came in…Weaver didn't.

Feeling confident that he had lost Weaver, Don got back on I-80 and continued to drive west. Coming over the rise was the Crown Vic proceeding in an easterly direction towards him.

Don was sweating, becoming dizzy and nauseated. He had to get off the highway or be discovered. **Wagonhound** appeared in the windshield. He guided the van off the exit. Not noticing the rest area, he pulled the van off the side of the ramp. He grabbed the knapsack on the passenger side floor. He had forgotten about the cooler which was still there on the seat—open with the carton of orange juice he was drinking at the monument sitting inside. After grabbing the forty-five from under the driver's seat and stuffing it in the knapsack, he stumbled from the van. *They will be here soon. I have to keep going.*

No where to go. The snow was lightly falling. There was no choice but to run out onto the prairie.

CHAPTER FIFTY TWO

Exhausted, Kathy and Mrs. Kendall returned to the Holiday Inn in Rawlins. It was late. Darkness had fallen hours earlier. Returning to their room, Mary had arrived first and was lying on the bed resting. Kathy in came in a few minutes later carrying her purse in one hand and her brother's brown brief case in the other.

They talked at length about their experiences over the last two days. Kathy shared how lucky she was to find Don's briefcase at the museum. Mary recounted her visit to the psychic and her vision that Don was still alive. She strongly believed that he could be somewhere ill or injured, unable to seek help.

Kathy put the briefcase flat on the bed. She pulled the chrome latch on one side to see if it would open. The briefcase wasn't locked. She opened the other latch and opened the lid. They apprehensively looked inside. Scattered in the bottom were several ball point pens and a couple pencils. There was yellow legal pad with notes written on it and loose papers which lay pinned underneath.

Kathy picked the pad up and scanned the pages.

"These are notes of his research for the book he was writing about the assassination."

She handed the pad to her mother who began to read the first page. She took out what looked like a photocopy of a ledger from the White House in 1862. It was fifteen pages of items purchased over a year. Don had highlighted several items of expensive jewelry, dresses, and other items of clothing. Also highlighted several times was camphorated opium tincture.

"There are quite a few expensive items here, even in monetary sums of those days. Have you ever heard of camphorated opium tincture?"

"No, Mary replied… but if it has opium in it there is a possibility it could have been a medicine."

Mary then took out copies of a perfectly written three page guest list with dates and payment amounts neatly written next to them.

"This looks like records from Mary Saratt's boarding house on H Street, Northwest in Washington D.C. They're dated November and December of 1864."

Mary took out another photocopy. It was of a letter dated November 2, 1862 written to the first lady at the White House.

My Dearest Mrs. Lincoln:

I am known to you by my making your acquaintance in Washington at a reception you held at the Willard Hotel. I wish to correspond to you now to thank you for your hospitality and express my wish to continue a cordial relationship. My interest in this contact is for the benefit of your husband. I will contact you again more directly to discuss the matter further.

Yours truly,

Mary S.

CHAPTER FIFTY THREE

Matt Daniels has finished for the day on his job site in Medicine Bow. As the sun set, he drove his pick up back towards Casper. He spotted a man in a tan coat on the side of the road flagging him down. Daniels slowed and looked more closely at him. He was about his height and build holding a knapsack over his shoulder.

Daniels pulled over next to the man who came over and opened the driver's side door of the pick up.

"Hi, Don said. Thanks for stopping. My car broke down a ways back."

"Hop in," Daniels said, looking at the man.

"I'm headed east, back to Casper."

Don got in the truck and closed the door. Daniels inspected the hitch hiker as he spoke. He was in rough shape. Unshaven, he looked pale as if he had been sick. There was a sour odor about him.

His deep set blue eyes and light brown hair and mustache were like his. He couldn't believe the resemblance.

"Actually, I am headed that way," Don said, trying to sound sincere.

The two of them travelled as the sun set and darkness fell. At first silent, Daniels broke the ice.

"My name is Matt."

"Hello Matt, I'm …Don thought, *I can't give him my real name, I'm on the run…* Ron. "Where are you headed?"

"Casper… I own a trailer there," Daniels stated modestly.

"Where were you headed when you broke down?" he asked.

Don decided not to tell the truth to disguise his circumstances. He wasn't trusting anyone.

"I was going to Jackson to visit relatives when I took a wrong turn and got lost. My car is totally disabled. It looks like the engine just seized up. There is no point in going back without a towing it in."

"That's a bummer."

Daniels looked as if he was thinking over something for a while as he drove.

Then he said, "Since you're in a fix, why don't you stay at my place until you can get a garage to tow it."

Don looked relieved but protested a little. "I couldn't impose on you."

"It's alright… really."

"Thanks, I really appreciate it."

CHAPTER FIFTY FOUR

Weaver needed some help. He had lost Kendall. He didn't want to think about what would happen when his employers found out. Perhaps he shouldn't have tried to do it alone. Overconfidence brought him to this point. He cursed at his incompetence and bad luck.

He thought back to his days as a stockbroker. He was mostly happy, making respectable money and had a nice apartment in Manhattan. When he saw the opportunity to make millions, he couldn't pass it up. Over time he had gotten deeper and deeper. Now, there was no way out. If Kendall were to go to the police, he would spend many years in jail. He was repulsed as he thought about what happens in prison. He didn't want to be someone's bitch, performing perverted sex acts to keep from getting his throat cut.

Back at the Motel 6 where he had checked in, Weaver took out the article he had saved from the business section of the *New York Times*. The heading read: **Kendall Rising Star at Klein.** The brief article had a head shot picture embedded next to it. The article told the story of Kendall's successful rise in the advertising industry.

Weaver cut out the picture and went to the Motel 6 office and asked them to Zerox ten copies.

Kendall had to be eliminated. He knew too much.

CHAPTER FIFTY FIVE

Kathy decided to return home. She hadn't given up hope but was beginning to accept the possibility that they would not find Donny. She had spent as much time as she could in Wyoming. She had to get back to work and close some real estate sales that she had pending.

Mom would carry on. She was tenacious like a mother bear protecting her cubs. She would fight tooth and nail until all possibilities were exhausted.

Kathy returned her rental car and Mary gave her a ride to the airport. They hugged, said goodbye, and promised to keep in touch.

Mary drove over to see Sheriff Coburn. After taking the elevator upstairs, she entered the Sheriff's Office. She announced herself to the officer who was on duty and asked to see the sheriff.

Sheriff Coburn came out of his office walked over to the counter, and extended his hand.

"Hello Mrs. Kendall," he said smiling, trying to be cordial. "What can I do for you today?"

He acted as if the altercation that they had just a few days ago had never happened. Mary just stood there looking at him. She had no intention of shaking his hand or any other courtesy that would indicate a positive relationship.

"May I speak to you in your office?"

"Sure."

Coburn led her to the door and held it open for her. Mary sat down in a wooden chair with arms across from the desk. She gathered herself—trying not to explode in anger.

Her face turning red, she addressed him.

"Sheriff, my daughter informs me that the search she requested for my son by the Air National Guard was cancelled by you."

Sheriff Coburn stopped smiling.

"This is a matter for the police. Your daughter did not have any business going over my head. I didn't want any outside organization doing something we could do ourselves."

"Sheriff, your department has come up with nothing! I am convinced that my son is alive and out there somewhere. He could be in danger. It is likely someone has done something to him."

Coburn began to look annoyed. This woman was not going to give an inch.

"Did you know that we have had cases where people become disoriented because of the altitude and lose their way? We don't have any evidence of anything else."

"Sheriff, did you know that my son's van was broken into out there at the rest stop?"

"Why no, Mrs. Kendall," Coburn remarked, looking surprised.

"I really can't believe that way out there anyone would even notice it."

"Do you have any idea who would be so interested in the van that they would do that?"

"No… I can't even imagine. Was anything taken?"

"The only thing we could figure was his address book and perhaps some money."

"His address book… that's strange. Are you sure? Perhaps he took that with him," Coburn said sarcastically.

"I tell you what. I will look into this break-in and see if we can find out anything."

CHAPTER FIFTY SIX

The headlights illuminated the white siding of the trailer as Matt Daniels pulled into the driveway. "Well this is it," he said as he got out of the truck.

In the darkness, Don eased himself out of the vehicle and followed Daniels toward the trailer. Knowing the way, Daniels walked up the steps on the porch and was able to unlock the front door. Daniels found the porch light and flipped it on so that Don could find his way up the steps. They entered the living room of the mobile home.

"Take a load off. Make yourself at home."

Don let out a big breath, half from exhaustion and half from the pain in his back as he sat on the sofa in the living room. He took off his coat, put it on the arm of the couch and rested the knapsack on the floor. He took off his shoes and massaged his aching feet.

"Can I offer you a drink?"

"Sure, Don said."

"All I have is beer and iced tea," Daniels said after opening the refrigerator. Don's hands were still trembling a little and he desperately wanted some alcohol. His resolve and his experience of the last several days dissuaded him from accepting the beer.

"The iced tea will be fine."

"This is unsweetened, is that okay?"

"That's fine."

Daniels walked into the living room and handed Don a tall, glass of tea. He took the glass and drained it quickly.

"You must really be thirsty," Daniels observed.

Returning to the kitchen, he poured another glass from a pitcher. He returned and gave it to Don and sat next to him. After taking a swig of his beer, Daniels got up off the couch.

"I'll look for some bedding."

As he relaxed on the sofa, Don looked around. The place wasn't half bad. It was small but had the essentials. To his left was a black reclining chair. He thought for a moment about his own chair, and how it seemed so long ago that he was relaxing in it. Just twelve feet in front of him, was the small kitchen area with the dining room table leaves down, sitting to one side, with two chairs at the ends. There was counter with a toaster and cutting board. Next to it, a stove occupied the rest of the wall. A small window was next to the table which would provide a view of the front while eating there.

Daniels re-appeared from the back bedroom with a pillow and a blanket.

"This ought to do fine for you to sleep on the sofa tonight. You can take a shower if you want to." Daniels hadn't commented on the now more apparent foul odor his visitor gave off since they had entered the trailer.

216

"Thanks. I really appreciate it. You really saved me back there."

Daniels just nodded. He wasn't doing anything much. Although he survived prison by being as brutal as those he served time with, he really wasn't a bad guy.

Don went into the small bathroom to clean up before retiring for the night. He took off his shirt and looked in the mirror. *I look like shit* he thought to himself as he stared at the image. His face appeared thinner than he remembered. His skin had a pasty pallor and purplish bags had formed under his eyes.

Despair overcame him. He had become an addict. He couldn't deny it anymore. Tears streamed down Don's face as he continued to look in the mirror. He had deceived his family and friends, not allowing them to understand his emotional pain. He lied about his growing dependence on Demerol and alcohol. Desperate, he had used Quaaludes to deal with his growing anxiety and inability to sleep. He had killed a man, foolishly took on Marna's killers and he was probably going to die.

Composing himself, he took off his soiled tee shirt, jeans, socks and briefs then stepped in the shower. He stood in the hot water letting it sooth his aching body and renewing his will to go on.

After leaving the bathroom, Daniels handed him a freshly laundered white tee shirt and with it, a folded flannel shirt.

The next morning, Matt was getting ready and was preparing to leave for work. He looked at his guest sleeping on the couch. The man looked totally exhausted. He walked over to the couch and shook Don's shoulder.

"Ron…Ron." Don raised his head, looked in the direction of the man and squinted at him.

"I'm going to work. It doesn't look like you're in any kind of shape to get up. Why don't you rest up today and I will call the garage in town tomorrow."

Don lowered his head, closed his eyes, and immediately fell back to sleep.

CHAPTER FIFTY SEVEN

Mary Kendall was packing her suitcases in her motel room at the Holiday Inn. It was time to return to Salisbury. She had done all that she could out here on this trip. She could always return if any leads turned up.

Over the last two weeks, she had posters made up at a local print shop with Don's picture on them. A reward of five-thousand dollars was offered. Home and work contact telephone numbers for her and Kathy were listed. She went back to Elk Mountain, Sinclair, Hanna, Medicine Bow, Rock River, and even Rawlins in case Don had gotten that far west, to post them. She made sure the posters were placed everywhere people would notice—mom-and-pop grocery store walls, restaurant doors, barber shop windows and on the mirrors behind bar counters.

The Carbon County Police were of no help and, in fact, obstructed further investigation. Nothing was being done about her report that Don's van was broken into. For now, no further information was available, creating a need for her to stay.

Mary missed being in the comfort of her own home. She missed Maggie. She began to think about the enthusiastic greeting she would get when arriving there. With Maggie's tail whipping Mary's legs, Maggie would jump on Mary's stomach, lick her face with her pink, wet tongue and snuggle with her reddish-brown snout.

CHAPTER FIFTY EIGHT

Over the last week, Weaver and two employees of his security firm had canvassed the area showing the picture. At times, they encountered Mrs. Kendall's posters tacked in various places. Pretending to be working for the Kendalls, they sometimes touted the reward. A break came when one of them talked to a man working on a job site in Medicine Bow.

Russell James had worked for Stern Investment Group, providing security for two years after serving eight years in the Special Forces. He was hired by Stern to complement Weaver's lack of experience in operations-type situations.

As he drove to Medicine Bow, he thought about his confrontation with Kendall on Long Island. Kendall had been lucky the police had showed up. Russell felt fortunate to get away in the Buick. This time, things will be different.

He stopped at the **Wagon Wheel,** a local restaurant and showed the picture around. The place was basically a coffee shop with a counter and black covered swivel stools. There were a few small booths. At the lunch hour the place was full of customers, mostly from the work site.

After asking at the counter, Russell walked around going from booth to booth showing the picture.

"Does anyone know this guy?"

Men in dirty work clothes and western-style cowboy hats looked at him shaking their heads. Two booths down, a man with a full, brown beard, a red bandana and hair hanging down past his collar took the photo and inspected it.

The man looked at Russell suspiciously. "Yeah, I know him. He works on the same job as me."

"I would like to talk to him."

"Is he in some kind of trouble?" The bearded man said, not wanting to incriminate his co-worker. He knew that a lot of guys on that site had pasts that they did not want visited upon them.

"No, no. I work for his family from back east who have lost touch. His father is gravely ill and would like to see him before he dies. Where is the job site?"

Somewhat convinced, the local told him. "It's down two-twenty about two miles."

"Thanks," Russell said with a half smile.

Russell used the pay phone outside the restaurant to call Weaver. He arranged to meet him at the job site and drove his rental down Route 220. Meeting Weaver and another employee there, they inauspiciously looked around trying not to be spotted. Then Russell saw him standing next to a drilling rig observing its pumping motion.

When the crew knocked off at the end of the day, Russell observed Kendall getting into a pickup truck. He got into his 4X4 and waited. He kept an eye on the black F-150 truck as the other vehicles left the lot. The pickup was leaving and pulled onto Route 220. Russell pulled onto the two lane road and followed him from a distance.

CHAPTER FIFTY NINE

Russell sat in his truck a safe distance away from Matt Daniels trailer. Weaver and another security firm employee slowly approached in the Crown Vic. They had followed the black pickup to that location. They really couldn't understand it, but Don Kendall had driven there and apparently was staying at the place. All they knew was that they had found their man.

With the intention of surprising the occupant, they left their vehicles down the road two hundred yards away.

The men cautiously approached the trailer with their weapons drawn. They headed toward the only entrance, the front door. Lacking any vegetation for cover, they crossed the snow covered lawn totally in the open.

Standing in the kitchen next to the window, Daniels spotted the men fanning out and coming toward the front porch. He quickly grabbed the Winchester hunting rifle he kept leaning against the wall in the corner of the living room.

"Ron, you had better hide. There is going to be trouble!" He yelled.

Grabbing the knapsack from the couch, Don got up from the reclining chair and scurried to the back bedroom. He fumbled in the knapsack and pulled out the forty-five. He had it, just in case.

Daniels broke out the bottom of the front window with his rifle. He fired at Russell who rolled to the ground, the bullet missing him. Daniels found another target—the other dark haired security employee, and this time he hit his mark. Blood flew from his shoulder as the bullet hit and he went down.

There were too many of them. The intruders were on the front porch. Daniels moved into the corner of the living room next to the reclining chair. Bullets penetrated the front door and tore though the wood on the inside. Splinter fragments flew.

As Weaver kicked the door open, Russell came through, firing rapidly with his black, compact, Walther PPK-L handgun. Daniels got off a shot. Missing badly, it put a hole in the wall of the kitchen. Just then, Daniels was hit by a hail of gunfire. Several spots of blood appeared on his torso and he hit the floor hard.

Weaver came in the room and stood over the man. The man's was face down on the living room floor, the side of his brown hair was matted with blood, and his blue eyes looked in the far distance. The red liquid was streaming from his body and forming a spreading pool in the brown carpet.

Weaver smiled wryly. He had finally gotten Kendall.

Russell held his Walther with two hands, kicking the doors open, pointing it in each remaining room of the small trailer.

No one was there.

It wouldn't be long before neighbors heard the gunfire and would investigate the noise. Unlike New York City, people paid attention to such things.

Don crouched behind the trailer flattened next to back window he had climbed out of. His hands trembled as he held the forty-five poised to use it, if necessary. After the shooting started, he knew better than to face such an overwhelming force.

He waited for what seemed to be an eternity. He heard footsteps throughout the trailer. They were searching it. At last, there were footsteps on the porch and on the stairs. In front, the vehicles' engines started up. They were leaving. Don breathed a sigh of relief.

CHAPTER SIXTY

Detective Sanderson was about to meet his new partner. He still missed Ricky.

Detective Richard Sambora was his friend and could always be counted on, no matter what. He had a wife, two kids and at the age of thirty-eight he was gone much too early. At first, Sanderson blamed himself. He didn't see it coming. The shooting had been a simple Kwick Mart store robbery in Queens. They were in the area and answered a back-up call. The shooter was waiting behind a car as they approached the parking lot.

The images of his mangled body after taking a shotgun blast lingered in his mind for months. Eventually, he had to let it go. The guilt, no matter how displaced, was tearing him up. There was nothing anyone could have done.

This morning he arrived at the station and as usual, fetched a cup of coffee from the squad room. Coming out of Lieutenant Stone's office was a woman heading for his office with the short, balding Lieutenant following.

Sanderson stared. He was getting a woman partner? A traditional guy, he didn't think women should be cops. They belonged at home, or perhaps working as a bank teller—but as a police detective in Homicide?

Sanderson retreated toward his office around the corner. The woman walked towards him. She was relatively tall, for a woman. She was a well built five-nine, with shortly styled dark brown hair and large brown eyes. She was wearing a loosely-fitting brown sport coat and black slacks. The Lieutenant stood next to Sanderson with the woman next to him.

"Detective Sanderson, this is Detective Barbara Levering."

The woman extended her large hand.

"Good to meet you," she said in an uncharacteristically soft voice. Judging her appearance, Sanderson thought her voice would a more man-like quality. Still staring, Sanderson reluctantly grasped her hand.

"Hello… I guess you are my new partner."

"That's the way it looks," she said sarcastically.

Completing his task, the Lieutenant went back to his office.

Barbara Levering has come up though the ranks over the last six years. She was one of the few recruits in the NYPD and had made an impression. In a hostage crisis, she had successfully been able to take down the suspect and had secured the release of the employees of a bank.

Barbara pulled out the chair and sat down at the desk across from Sanderson. She placed the small cardboard box she was carrying on the desktop. Sanderson looked at her, sipping coffee out of his green and white Marine Corps mug.

"Since we are going to be working together, should I call you Barbara or do you prefer Detective Levering?"

"I prefer Barbara, and don't worry, I'll be fine working in Homicide."

"Well...I hope so. I could really use a partner.

CHAPTER SIXTY ONE

Sheriff Coburn and Rod Jones headed out to a trailer park in Casper, thirty miles north. The call had come in earlier that day. A neighbor had reported gun shots coming from the direction of a trailer owned by a Matt Daniels. They said that one sounded like a rifle shot, but there were many other gunshots not usual for hunters. They reported that it sounded like there was a war going on.

Coburn had gotten calls from well meaning residents in the past. These trailer parks are in isolated areas, not far from where elk hunting took place. The whole thing usually turned out to be a false alarm.

The green and white cruiser pulled up the driveway of Daniels' trailer. It was quiet. There were no vehicles parked anywhere, not even in the driveway. Coburn and Johnson walked up to the front porch. Multiple bullet holes had shattered the front door. There were others in the white siding and shell casings were spread out on the porch and steps. The front window was broken out.

Now alarmed, the officers un-holstered their large-barreled revolvers and held them out defensively as they quickly walked up the steps onto the porch. Arriving at the door, they splayed themselves on each side of it, making sure that they were not targets.

Coburn pushed open the bullet riddled door which flopped on its hinges as it flew open. He ducked his head around the door frame and took a cautious look inside. The living room and kitchen area were empty. From his vantage point he saw blood on the floor and more shell casings. Down the small hallway no one stirred. The whole place was eerily quiet.

Coburn nodded in the direction of the door and the two officers quickly entered the trailer in a crouched position with their guns drawn. Jones moved down the hall and checked the other rooms just in case. The place was empty.

Coburn continued to investigate. It appeared that a person had been shot and had been bleeding badly. He crouched down studying the large, dark red pool that had collected in the brown carpet. A .22 Winchester rifle lay next to the reclining chair. Bullets had penetrated the wall opposite the door. There was a hole in the wall and glass in the kitchen area.

"There must have been one hell of a fire fight here," he finally said as Jones joined him in the living room.

"Someone was badly wounded, maybe killed… but no body," Deputy Jones observed.

"I wonder who would cause all this destruction way out here."

CHAPTER SIXTY TWO

Judith DePetro arrived home to her apartment in Mid-Manhattan after a long day. She had just come back from a trip to Saint Thomas in the Virgin Islands. She had spent four wonderful weeks there. It was a beautiful tropical island with small beaches—sculpted, rocky hills rising above them with iguanas basking in the sun. She had stayed at Bolongo Bay Resort, which featured underwater diving lessons and a tennis club.

She sat down to relax on the sofa, took off her Reebok running shoes and discarded them on the carpeted floor. Two suit cases still sat on the floor of the living room. She hadn't bothered to unpack. After sitting down, she spotted the red indicator on her answering machine showing two messages.

She pressed the play button. A male voice came on.

"I really would like to speak to you. Please call me at three-oh-seven, three-two-eight, four-three-six five."

There was a pause and the call ended with a click. The voice sounded familiar, but strange. The person must have had her unlisted number. It sounded a little like Don, but did it? She wasn't sure. She hadn't talked to Don since he left for Wyoming. She had received a postcard from Chicago to inform her that the trip was going well. She missed him and longed for the day he would return. The other message was from an old friend she knew in college.

Judith jotted down the numbers on the back of an unopened piece of mail and mechanically pressed the erase button. She picked up the phone and dialed the numbers the unidentified person left. She let it ring on the other end for seven or eight times hoping she would hear Don's voice. No one picked up and there wasn't a voice mail message.

CHAPTER SIXTY THREE

Dan Blackman walked into the NYPD homicide office. Sanderson and Levering were expecting him.

He walked normally and appeared generally in good physical condition but there was an odd appearance about his face. After his brawl with Kendall, he had hit his head on a table and could have been killed. Fortunately, he had survived. Although he did not know it, concerned residents of the Falstaff Apartment complex had called for help. It was touch and go. At one point he died but with persistence, the paramedics had kept him alive.

There was one catch—he was in a comatose state for a month. When he awoke he was generally not affected by the blow to his head with one exception, one side of his face was partially paralyzed.

Now that he was offered a deal to clear him of any charges, he was going to tell the cops everything he knew.

After inquiring about the case, Blackman was escorted to the interview room. It had the sweet, antiseptic smell of air freshener, courtesy of Detective Levering. After sitting down at the stainless steel table the two detectives entered the room and greeted him.

"Mr. Blackman, I'm Detective Sanderson," he said extending his hand and grasping the other man's. "This is detective Levering."

Levering nodded cordially.

They sat down across from their witness.

"We asked you to come in to clear some things up for us. As you know, we are investigating Marna Anderson's murder. We understand that you knew her."

Blackman nervously ran his fingers through his black, curly hair. He spoke out of the left side of his mouth.

"Lithen, I want your assurance that I will be protected," he said with a mild, but noticeable slur.

"If they get wind of this, my life could be in danger."

"By *they* do you mean Weaver's organization?"

"Yeah…they probably don't know that I am alive. If they found out that I talked, there could be trouble."

"Don't worry Mr. Blackman, you will be protected," Levering said, her large brown eyes showing concern.

"How did you know Marna Anderson?"

"I met her through a friend and we went out a couple times. I introduced her to John Weaver who was a stockbroker. Marna had a job at another firm. She was giving me information about that firm's acquisitions and trades and I would pass it on to him."

"Did you know why Ms. Anderson was killed?" Sanderson inquired.

"No… but it could be because of her knowledge of the insider trades. She might have gotten scared as the investigation by the SEC got closer."

"How well did you know Ralph Augustine and Matthew Simms who made trades based on the information of Weaver?"

"I didn't know them. I just passed the information to Weaver."

"Did you know Don Kendall?"

"Not until he confronted me. He found out about my association with Marna and John and thought I was involved with her murder. Believe me… I had nothing to do with it.

Sanderson paused for effect.

"Do you know who did it?"

Blackman looked at Sanderson soberly.

"I honestly don't know…but I suspect that Simms' firm had something to do with it. John became a loose cannon trying to protect them after being made head of security."

"Do you think his employees killed her?"

"Like I said, I think they may have done it…Weaver told me they were going to try and talk some sense into her."

Sanderson decided to change directions.

"Is there anyone else that could be personally involved? Anyone that either Marna Anderson or Don Kendall knew that could be connected to the case?"

"Kendall had a co-worker… Judith something. I don't remember her last name. I never met her but Marna told be that she was Don's best friend at work."

"Was she romantically involved with Don Kendall," Levering interjected.

"I don't know, but probably not. Kendall was deeply in love with Marna. If there was a relationship, it was before he met Marna."

CHAPTER SIXTY FOUR

Judith DePetro sat in a gray metal chair at the stainless steel table in the dingy green interrogation room waiting for the two detectives. She wore a casual red dress with black flecks in it, the neck open exposing her newly acquired tan. On the white collar of her dress was a silver pin in which the initials JAD were engraved. Her shiny, brown hair was tied in a bun as she customarily wore it. Judith's fingers nervously fidgeted with an empty styrofoam coffee cup, breaking small pieces off the edge.

The detectives entered the room, each holding a cup of coffee. Sanderson also held a Manila file folder as he sat down across from Judith. Detective Levering took a chair beside her. Judith looked across the table at Sanderson's deeply lined face. His brown, penetrating eyes seemed to drill through her skull. He spoke as he glanced at the open file on the table.

"Miss DePetro, I am Detective Sanderson and this is Detective Levering," he said with a half smile.

"We have brought you here to investigate the murder of Marna Anderson. We have learned from a witness that you knew her."

Judith looked at him quizzically. "I wondered why you called me down here."

"I only met her once. She was dating Don Kendall. Other than that, I just knew *of* her. Don told me about her murder. He was quite upset."

"How well did you know Donald Kendall?"

"I worked with him for seven years. We were good friends."

"Did you know he was missing?"

"Missing... I had no idea, she said, looking disturbed. I just got back from vacation. There was a phone call on my answering machine which sounded like it could have been Don...but the person didn't identify himself. They left a phone number."

"Do you know where the phone call came from?"

"No. I tried to call back, but there was no answer."

"Can you tell me when Don disappeared?" Judith said, concerned.

"Four weeks ago."

Judith began to tear up. She couldn't believe it.

"You two must have been close," Levering said, touching her forearm sympathetically.

"Yes, we were the best of friends," Judith said looking down at the table.

"Have you ever been to Miss Anderson's apartment?" Levering continued.

"No. Like I said... I didn't know her that well," she said nervously.

"Our source tells us that you knew the victim more than you are telling us."

Sanderson picked up the questioning, this time his voice was more intimidating.

"Are you sure that you have never been to her apartment?"

Judith responded defensively. "Like I have already told you... no."

"Can you account for your whereabouts on November eleventh two years ago?

"Two years ago?... I really can't remember. That was a long time ago. I was probably at home."

"Was anyone with you?" Sanderson said, pressing the point.

"Probably not... but I'm not sure. I will have to think about it. Am I in some kind of trouble?"

"There is no reason to worry. We're just following up on the leads that we have developed recently."

"Can you tell me anything about Don's disappearance?" Judith asked.

"We don't know much... just that he disappeared in Wyoming," Sanderson replied.

"I knew that he was going on a trip out there. What do you think happened to him?"

"I'm afraid that we don't know at this point."

The two detectives stood up from the table.

"Miss Depetro thanks for coming in. We really appreciate your cooperation. We will keep in touch," Sanderson said.

As Judith exited the room, Levering closed the door and looked at Sanderson.

"Do you believe her?"

"No, but at this point we have no evidence she is involved."

CHAPTER SIXTY FIVE

A week later, Kathy was back at her home in Woodbine Maryland. She had not heard anything from her mother about any new information concerning Don's disappearance.

Although she thought about it each day, she had returned to her routine. The real estate market was heating up. She was busy.

One day at work, Kathy's mother called.

"Kathy," Mrs. Kendall said with urgency.

"Someone used Donny's phone card to make a call."

Taken aback, Kathy sat down at her desk. "From where?"

"From Washington State."

"How did you find out?"

"I got a bill in the mail."

"Washington State? Do you think it was Donny?"

Kathy began to think about the possibilities.

"Someone could have found or stolen the card and used it."

Mary paused for a moment.

"I guess that is possible too. I was hoping that it could be Donny. It would be an indication that he is still alive."

"Do you think there is any way to find out who made the call?"

"You could try calling the number listed," Kathy suggested.

"Okay, let me try now. I'll call you back."

While looking at the billing statement, Mary dialed the number charged to the credit card. It rang—one... two... three... four... five....six....seven times. No one answered. She tried again. Six more rings. No one picked up.

Kathy's office phone rang again.

"Kathy, there is no one answering at that number."

"Perhaps it is a phone booth or a place where no one is at home. Mom, we can hope."

"Washington State is a long way from Wyoming," Mary observed.

"I could try it again this evening. If Donny could make it that far, why wouldn't he try to contact us?"

"You're right ...maybe it wasn't Donny but where would someone else get his phone card?"

"I don't know, but I hope they didn't steal it from him. I think about him everyday and hope that he is okay. Mom, I am busy at work. I'll call you when I get home. I love you. Talk to you soon. Bye."

CHAPTER SIXTY SIX

Detectives Sanderson and Levering decided to call is Matthew Simms. He was currently out on bail until his trial which had been postponed for weeks. The prosecution had a very strong case on the charges, which had resulted from his illegal trading of hedge funds. Blackman had confirmed his firm's involvement in Marna Anderson's murder and they wanted to turn up the heat.

Matthew Simms was already seated with the two detectives in the interview room. His tall frame filled the metal chair as his long legs extended beneath the table. His face was lined and showed years of worry and his gray temples framed deep lines in his forehead.

Sanderson started the questioning. He had been suspecting Simms's involvement since questioning him at his house on Long Island which now seemed like several years ago. Simms had brought his attorney. The dapper looking man sat next to him facing the two detectives.

"Mr. Simms, I wanted to talk to you again in regard to my murder investigation. You can make it easy on yourself or we can use the evidence we now have to charge you as an accessory to murder. Do you know what that would mean?"

Simms looked at Sanderson worriedly.

"I'm not sure, but it doesn't sound good. I have already been indicted for securities fraud and will likely be convicted. I didn't think things could be any worse."

"Well, you're wrong. We have a witness who will connect you to the activities of your security firm headed by John Weaver. They are directly involved in Marna Anderson's murder and they worked for you! That makes you an accessory and you can be charged."

"Look...they worked for me but I didn't know anything about any murder."

"If you cooperate, I will talk to the District Attorney about lessoning any charges."

Simms leaned his head next to his lawyer's and murmured some questions. Seeming to attain the direction he was looking for, he appeared ready.

"Okay, I can answer some questions if I get immunity. I don't want any murder charges and nothing I say here will be used in the SEC investigation."

"Mr. Simms, I can't vouch for the SEC. I am only interested in the murder. Like I said, I will talk to the D.A., depending on the extent of the information you provide."

Simms nodded his approval.

Looking imposingly at Simms, Sanderson was ready for some hard questions.

"Did you have Miss Anderson and Don Kendall followed?"

"Yes... but that was just to keep tabs on them. I didn't want her to tell anyone about the information we were getting."

"You got the information from Marna Anderson, didn't you?"

"Look… I really don't want to implicate myself any further. I swear, I was not aware of any murder."

Sanderson was becoming annoyed. "Mr. Simms, answer the question. You need to cooperate to have any chance of a deal."

"Did Marna Anderson provide information from her firm to you?"

Simms again looked at his lawyer who nodded. "Yes, but I am not providing specifics about the information."

"Did you employ John Weaver, Samuel Jenkins and others to harass and threaten Marna Anderson and Don Kendall?"

"I don't know about threaten… but yes, I had them followed. Like I said, I did not order nor was I involved in any murder."

Sanderson wasn't satisfied.

"Have you communicated with John Weaver recently?" Simms looked at his lawyer who nodded in agreement.

"He called me two days ago."

"Where is he?" Sanderson demanded.

"He is staying at an apartment house in Queens."

"Mr. Simms, don't leave town. I may have some other questions for you. For the time being, you are free to go. The D.A. will be in touch about your testimony."

Smiling, Sanderson nodded to Levering who knew that they were about to arrest Weaver.

CHAPTER SIXTY SEVEN

Kathy was at home watching television in her living room when the telephone rang. She got up and grabbed the handset on an end table next to the sofa.

"Hello," Kathy said, half cheerfully.

"Hi Kathy, this is Nancy McGrath."

Kathy had known Nancy from their membership in the Lincoln Society. Both she and Don had been members for years.

"Hi Nancy, how are you?"

"I'm doing fine Kathy." She paused.

"I heard about Don's disappearance...I am very sorry. He is a great guy."

"The reason I am calling is that I may have seen him at a symposium in Springfield."

Kathy was dumbfounded.

"He has been missing for five weeks now. Do you really think it was him?"

"This guy really looked a lot like him. When I saw him walking down the hall in a crowd outside of the hotel auditorium, I followed him."

"Did you talk to him," Kathy said excitedly.

"I'm sorry Kathy. He got lost in the crowd. I even checked to see if he had registered... no luck. I thought that you would like to know. I called because I thought that any information you had might help you find him."

"Nancy, I really wish you had spoken to him. At this point, I believe there is still a great possibility he is alive. We can hope. Thanks for calling."

After hanging up, Kathy sat on the sofa and stared at the television and reflected on the information she had just received. Could it be Donny? It didn't make sense. If he was alive and at that conference, why hadn't he tried to contact her? A phone call, postcard—anything.

CHAPTER SIXTY EIGHT

The cold December air blew against the windshield of Sanderson's black cruiser as he and his new partner drove to Queens. After crossing the East River Bridge, they traveled several miles past modest, compact individual houses with small yards. Snow covered the lawns and was piled up along the curbs and next to the sidewalks leading to the front doors.

After turning onto Conduit Avenue which became Laurelton Parkway, they made a left onto Merrick Boulevard. Down the residential street they looked for the address Simms had provided. They found the house on the right. The house was larger than the others on the block and was divided into apartments. Parked in front were several types of cars. The Crown Vic Sanderson had encountered months earlier was no where on the street. He didn't think that it would be. The vehicle was never found after the APB he has put out on it. They had found the Buick LeSabre abandoned the next day.

"So... Weaver has decided to hide in the midst of the suburbs," Sanderson observed.

Once finding the address Simms gave them, they parked a few doors down from the house. They got out of the car and approached the front door of a three story frame house with brown shingles. After checking the numbers on the mailbox, they found the one they were looking for. Weaver's apartment was up the stairs on the side of the building.

"You cover the front. In case he decides to come out through the house that way," he said to Levering.

Careful not to alarm his suspect, Sanderson quietly walked up the stairs. He approached a side entrance door with a small roof covering it. Sanderson peered in a small glass window at the top of the door which revealed the kitchen of the apartment. He hammered on the door.

"John Weaver, this is the police. We want to talk to you." The place was quiet. Maybe he wasn't home.

"Open up or we'll come in."

Sanderson hesitated a minute and kicked the door. At first it resisted but with a second kick it caved in and flew open. Sanderson stayed low with his Police Special drawn as he quickly entered the kitchen. A bullet whizzed past his head and slammed into a dish cabinet behind him. Sanderson hit the floor with his weapon pointing toward the small dining area beyond. Weaver must have been behind a wall separating the dining area from another room. He fired again. Splintered wood flew, and dishes shattered as the bullet just missed Sanderson again hitting a lower cabinet.

Hearing the gun shots, Levering quickly climbed the stairs. As she arrived on the porch, she saw Sanderson pinned on the kitchen floor. She stood with her weapon drawn just outside the door. Weaver peeked out behind the wall revealing his right side. Levering stepped into the kitchen, fired and caught Weaver in the shoulder. He reeled back. Sanderson was quickly on him and pointed his weapon at Weaver's chest.

"Drop it."

Weaver complied.

Sanderson stood across from his assailant holding his shoulder and wincing in pain.

Levering took out her handcuffs, turned Weaver around and clicked them on his wrists.

"You are under arrest."

Sanderson looked at his new partner. "Good work detective," he said approvingly.

Detective Sanderson and Levering brought Weaver into the precinct for questioning and advised him of his rights. Levering gave him first aid for the flesh wound in his right shoulder. Weaver sat at the table of the interview room holding his shoulder with his hand. His bloodstained empty gray silk shirt sleeve hung with his bandaged arm resting inside.

Weaver's face had a pained expression as he strained to tolerate his throbbing shoulder. His long blond hair was stylishly cut and well kept. He was shaven and this skin appeared unblemished except for the small cyst protruding right next to his left eyebrow.

Detective Sanderson sat down at the table across from him. He looked angry, just barely able to contain himself. Leaning into the table, his eyes glared at Weaver as he addressed him.

"Mr. Weaver, you know that you are in a lot of trouble. You are being charged with eluding a police pursuit on Long Island, reckless endangerment, resisting arrest, attempted murder of a police officer and you are a suspect in the murder of Marna Anderson. It would be in your best interest if you would cooperate."

"Please, you have to take me to a hospital," Weaver said, making an effort to tolerate the pain.

"I really need to get this shoulder treated. It really hurts."

Sanderson ignored him. "Mr. Weaver we will get to that."

"Do you know a man named Sam Jenkins? "

"Yes, he worked for Simms."

"What did he do?"

"He was hired to provide security for Stern Investments."

"Were you in charge of the security firm?"

"Yes... please get me to a hospital," Weaver said squirming in his chair.

"Don't worry, we will...just answer a few more questions."

"Did you attempt to kill Don Kendall on Long Island eighteen months ago?"

"Yes, yes."

"We have a witness who will testify that you, Simms and Augustine made illegal trades on the stock market. Did you kill Marna Anderson in an effort to cover up those illegal trades?"

"No," Weaver retorted, this time ignoring the pain.

"We were following her and Kendall but we didn't kill her," Weaver spat though his clenched teeth.

Detective Levering then entered the room. She glared at Sanderson sitting there with this wounded suspect.

"Detective Sanderson, I think this man needs to go to the hospital. We ought to end any further questioning." Sanderson looked at his partner angrily for interrupting him.

"Detective, if you insist, we can get him treated. Weaver, we can pick this up when you return."

Levering took Weaver out of the room to meet the police officers ready to take him the emergency room.

Out in the squad room, Levering and Sanderson discussed the case. Sanderson was now convinced that either Weaver or one of his employees had killed Anderson.

"I think Weaver is guilty as hell. Both he and Jenkins admitted to being at the apartment. Even if they did not intend to kill her, they could have by accident."

Levering looked at it with a fresh set of eyes. "You may be right, but they both tell the same story. Judith DePetro is another good possibility. Our eyewitness puts her at the scene."

CHAPTER SIXTY NINE

Judith was again sitting in the interview room. She was beginning to worry about what the police suspected. She had thought about hiring a lawyer but decided that she didn't need to. Other than her association with Don and the fact that she had met Marna, she had no connection to the case. She had taken off from work at Klein for the second time and hoped that this would be the last time she was in this place.

Detectives Levering and Sanderson entered the room.

"Good morning Ms. DePetro," Levering said with a smile.

"Thanks for coming in. We have a few more questions to help us with the investigation of Marna Anderson's murder," she said, as she sat down at the table across from Judith.

Sanderson sat next to Levering. He placed a plastic envelope marked **evidence** and a file folder on the table.

"What's this about? Didn't I answer your questions the last time? Am I in trouble?"

"I appreciate your cooperation thus far, Ms. Depetro but some things have come to our attention which we need to ask you," Levering said in a conciliatory tone. "I need to tell you that anything you may say will be used against you in a court of law." She proceeded to go though the other rights.

"Actually, we wanted to ask you about your relationship with Don Kendall. Were you romantically involved?"

"Why, no... I do miss him terribly...but like I said before, we were just good friends," Judith said looking self conscious.

"Are you sure that you have never been to Marna Anderson's apartment?"

"No...I haven't." Judith was beginning to get defensive.

"We have an eyewitness who saw you there. A neighbor across the hall heard all the commotion and looked out in the hall. She saw you leaving that day wearing a man's overcoat and hat."

Sanderson brought out the envelope and slid the contents on the table in front of her. A ladies watch with a broken red leather band lay on the table.

"Is this your watch?"

Judith looked at the new watch on her arm. "No...I...I lost my watch but that's not it."

"I think this is yours," Levering said.

"This is an unusual make of watch...a Steinhausen. Are you sure that you have never owned a watch like this?"

"No, that is not mine," Judith said staring at the table.

"I think you are lying Ms. DePetro. We surveyed the city for purchases of this brand of watch. Do you know what we found? You bought this watch two years ago at a jewelry store on Fifth Avenue."

"You lost it at Ms. Anderson's apartment when you strangled her."

"Your fingerprints were also found at the apartment," Sanderson said pulling a copy of the prints from the file.

"Those can't be my prints."

"We obtained a search warrant to get prints from your apartment and we compared those to the one's we found."

Judith looked stunned. Trembling, she stared at the items on the table not knowing what to say. Tears slowly came to her eyes. She began to sob uncontrollably. Levering moved to the chair next to her and put her arm around Judith.

"I loved him," she blubbered.

"That woman was going to take him away. He didn't realize how much I cared...he couldn't see it. She was just going to dump him anyway. She was seeing that guy, Dan.

"So you went to the apartment that day after you saw the men leave," Sanderson said.

Judith composed herself. "Yes. The place was already a mess. She was lying on the floor. I thought she was dead. She asked me to help her. Then I did it."

"Do you mean choked her?"

"Yes, I...I strangled her...and ran out as fast as I could."

"That's right Ms. DePetro, and you knocked over Don Kendall on the way out."

CHAPTER SEVENTY

Detectives Sanderson and Levering sat drinking cups of coffee in the small office they occupied. An extra desk for Levering had been placed facing Sanderson's.

"I talked to a friend in the State's Attorney's office. Judith DePetro has been indicted and her trial is about to begin," Sanderson commented.

"When is it going to start," Levering replied.

"He thinks next week."

"It should be a slam dunk case considering the evidence we have… and her confession," Levering surmised.

"Yeah, that confession was the icing on the cake. You did a great job interviewing her."

"Thanks. You weren't bad yourself," she said smiling.

"Have you heard anything about John Weaver's case?"

"He's in deep shit with the Securities and Exchange Commission. He was convicted along with Simms and Augustine for five counts of securities fraud and eight counts of wire fraud. They combined the charges and were given three years for each count, a total of fifteen years in prison. With our office, he was indicted for resisting arrest, reckless endangerment and attempted murder of a police officer. He was given twenty-five years for the attempted murder charge and the other lesser charges were dropped.

Sam Jenkins and Simms have testified against Weaver in the reckless endangerment and assault of Don Kendall and Marna Anderson. According to our deal, Simms will get immunity but Jenkins will only be charged with resisting arrest and because of his cooperation, the reckless endangerment and handgun charges will be dropped."

"What about Simms involvement in Anderson's death?"

"Since Weaver's men did not kill her, he has not been charged with conspiracy to commit murder."

Looking at Levering, Sanderson smiled. "Barbara, you were right. I was sure that he ordered a hit on her, but he didn't."

CHAPTER SEVENTY ONE

Sam Williams parked his silver Ford pickup on the street next to the white court house in Rawlins. It had been seven months since Don Kendall had disappeared. Williams took the elevator up to the sheriff's office. He walked though the door and up to the front counter.

"I have to report something to Sheriff Coburn."

The sheriff came out of his office and walked up to the front. "You were looking for me?"

"Yeah sheriff, my buddy and me found the remains of a man's body when I was out huntin' yesterday."

"Are you sure it is human?"

"Yeah, there isn't much left, but it is definitely looks like a man."

"Where?"

"I was out near Hanna, south of Route 30 about one hundred yards from the road."

"Was there anything on the body to identify him?'

The hunter took out a social security card and two credit cards and placed them on the counter.

"The stuff I found says Donald Kendall."

Coburn picked up the cards and examined them. "This is someone we have been looking for. He went missing out I-80 a few months back. He had pulled off the Wagonhound exit and left his van there. Can you take me to the spot?"

"Sure, I remember where it is."

Coburn turned toward the deputy's desk. "Deputy Jones, let's take a ride."

The two police officers exited the building and got into Jones' cruiser. The officers followed the truck out to I-80 for a few miles and took Route 30 north. As they approached Hanna, the truck pulled over and the police car followed, parking on the side of the road. The hunter got out of his pickup and the officers followed suit.

They walked over the prairie a few feet. The terrain was mostly flat. The prairie grass covering it had turned green. Crops of rocks were dispersed here and there. Clumps of trees appeared on the horizon.

"This is where we were hunting."

"There he is," Williams said, pointing to the spot.

Coburn walked up to the remains. The corpse was badly deteriorated by the elements and picked clean by wildlife. The remnants of a brown coat clung to the torso. A tattered pair of jeans and a pair of tennis shoes lay a few feet away. A tuft of brown hair still remained on the barren skull. An open, apparently empty, canteen lay next to the body.

Coburn walked over an examined the corpse and scanned the surrounding area. There were no signs anyone else human had been out there—but after this long, it wasn't likely any activity would still be evident.

"The poor guy. It looks like he did get lost."

After thanking the hunter, the officers returned to the office. Coburn sat at his desk and dialed the phone number he had written on a note pad for Mary Kendall. After a few rings she answered.

"Mrs. Kendall?"

"Yes, this is Mary Kendall."

"This is Sheriff Coburn."

"Sheriff, I didn't expect you to call…is there any news about my son?"

"Mrs. Kendall, I'm afraid it is not good. We found some remains out on the prairie close to Route 30 which appear to be your son."

Mary sounded skeptical. "Are you sure?"

"We found a social security card and two credit cards which have his name on them. It is very likely. Does he own a brown winter coat?"

"Yes he does. Why?"

"There was part of a coat on the remains."

"Did you find anything else which would tell you what happened and how he got there?"

"No. I'm afraid not. There is no evidence of foul play. Otherwise, we don't know for sure. He must have gotten lost and walked to that spot, we don't know."

Mary paused to gather herself. The realization that her son could actually be dead struck her. "Where are these remains now?"

"We are having them taken to the hospital in Cheyenne which has a medical examiner. He will make a determination of the identity of the remains and perform an autopsy to find the cause of death. Can you get Donald's dental records for a comparison and send them out?"

"I will ask my daughter to handle that. She will have to get them from New York where he lived. I will have her send them as soon as possible."

"Thank you Mrs. Kendall."

The sheriff hung up.

CHAPTER SEVENTY TWO

Kathy called the Cheyenne medical examiner's office. She had located and sent Donny's dental records ten days earlier. She thought that given the population of the area, they must not have many cases. A clerk answered the phone.

"Medical examiner's office," she said in a monotone.

"This is Kathy Wayne. I am calling to find out the results of the dental comparison of the remains sent by the Carbon County Sheriff's Department."

The woman's voice became more cheery.

"Yes, Mrs. Wayne...I remember receiving your records. Hold on, I'll check."

The clerk put the phone down on the desk for a few minutes. Kathy could hear the sound of file drawers opening and slamming shut.

"I can't seem to locate that file," she said, appearing flustered.

"If you will give me more time, I will check again."

"Sure, take your time."

After holding for twenty minutes, the clerk got back on the phone with Kathy.

"It appears that the file has been misplaced or lost."

"What about the autopsy results?"

"Usually, they are kept in the same file."

Kathy couldn't believe it. "This is ridiculous. I want to talk to the medical examiner."

"Hold on and I'll see if he is available."

The clerk left for a few minutes and came back to the telephone. "He's not available right now. I will have him call you back."

Two hours later, the medical examiner called Kathy.

"Miss Kendall, this is Dr. Lee returning your call."

"Dr. Lee, I was told by your clerk that my brother, Donald Kendall's file has been lost. Is that true?"

The medical examiner held the phone as he paused. "Miss Kendall...this is very unusual. We have a small office here. This never happens...I thoroughly checked our records...it just isn't there. I'm sorry."

Appalled, Kathy hung up the phone. How could those records be "lost"? There is something more at work here.

CHAPTER SEVENTY THREE

Don was sitting in a coffee shop in Jackson, Wyoming. The place had booths against one wall and the rest of the room had small circular tables with comfortable chairs dispersed around them. The familiar aroma of coffee brewing and breakfast food cooking reminded him of Michael's Café on Madison Avenue.

While sipping a cup of coffee, he thought about how totally at peace he was. Drug free, his mind was clear. At times, craving gnawed at him, which he was able to resist. He had come to the realization that he had developed an addiction to Demerol. He had learned that it was an opiate, like heroin and the addiction potential was high. His drinking had made matters worse, creating a deepening dependency. Desperate for help, he began attending A.A. meetings. At first, he resisted the feeling that he belonged there. After a short time, he always attended the few meetings that were held in Jackson and found a sponsor.

He had gotten a part-time job at a local book store. It was the perfect job for him. He had always loved reading. It was slow paced, low profile, and he enjoyed interacting with the customers.

As winter turned to spring, then summer, he dealt with the back pain he experienced day by day. Daily yoga exercises and meditation gave him positive alternatives to any mind-altering substances.

While sipping his coffee, he looked down at the small circular table in front of him. There was a discarded, two week old copy of the *New York Times* newspaper. The headline caught his eye: **Convictions Made In Insider Trading Scheme**

Don continued to read the article.

The states attorney's office announced today that the State of New York had obtained the convictions of three major figures in the investigation, Matthew Simms, Ralph Augustine and John Weaver. The trial, which lasted for eight months, featured a major witness, Daniel Blackman who had first-hand knowledge of the scheme.

Blackman, who had been given immunity from prosecution, testified that he had been a provider of information between the firms of Wilson Jones and Stern Investment Group. The two firms conspired to use information about Hedge Funds to trade them illegally for huge profits.

Dan Blackman, Don thought. *He's still alive?* Don was relieved that he hadn't killed him, but a familiar feeling of guilt gnawed at him. He had run away to avoid being charged with murder. Despite his irresponsible behavior, Blackman had survived. He hadn't done anything to help him.

The article went on:

John Weaver, a defendant in the case, had been convicted of other related charges. He headed a security organization for Stern that had threatened and intimidated other individuals as part of a cover-up. Testifying against him in those charges were Matthew Simms and Sam Jenkins, an employee of Weaver.

"All right! That son-of-a-bitch Weaver is getting what he deserves," Don said to himself, gleefully banging the table with his fist and rattling his coffee mug. The few other customers momentarily turned to look at him.

As he stared at the newspaper, he began to think about Marna. He wondered if his efforts had led to Marna's killer or killers being brought to justice. From the new article, it appeared that no one was being tried for her murder. It wasn't even mentioned; just "threats and intimidation." He had not completed his task of finding her killer. He wondered. Who did kill Marna?

At least he had found Weaver and his hired goons. This forced them out in the open so that the police became aware of Weaver's wrongdoing. Now they were going to jail and he was out of danger.

Don decided that he had been in hiding long enough. It was time to take responsibility for what he had done to Blackman. He was going to contact his mother and sister to reveal himself and then call the police.

CHAPTER SEVENTY FOUR

Mary Kendall had just gotten home from work. As usual, Molly greeted her in an enthusiastic fashion. She would not have kept her sanity over these months without her.

The phone in the living room rang. These days, the calls were usually disappointing and sometimes depressing. She sighed and forced herself to answer.

"Hello," she said not putting much effort into the greeting.

"Mom?"

The voice was distant but very familiar. "Donny is that you?"

"Yes Mom," Don said, a little ashamed.

"Donny, is it really you! I knew you were alive." Tears of joy flowed down her cheeks as she spoke.

"Your sister and I have been worried sick. Young man if I wasn't so happy to hear from you, you would be in a lot of trouble, she said in an admonishing tone. Where have you been, and why didn't you call us? We spent weeks looking for you!"

"Right now I am in Jackson, Wyoming. Mom, it's a long story. All I can tell you is that I have been in trouble and I didn't want you endanger you and Kathy.

"What kind of trouble?"

"It was very serious. I'm sorry that I didn't try to get in touch with you. After Marna was murdered, I thought I had killed a man. I didn't know it, but it turns out that he is still alive. Not only that, I was threatened several times and was followed out here...I was so afraid, I had to run and hide."

"We found your van out off that exit and we were hopeful. Then the sheriff called saying that they had found your remains."

"I'm sorry you had to go through that Mom."

"Donny, it sounds like you have been through quite an ordeal. Are you still in danger?"

"No. I just read in the newspaper that people responsible are in custody."

"Where, in New York?"

"Yes, I will tell you all about it later."

"Donny I'm so glad that you are alive—I guess I will forgive you for deceiving us. When are you coming home?"

"Mom, I need to take care of some things. I'll be home in two weeks. Can you pick me up at BWI?"

"Of course. I can't wait to call Kathy and tell her. Call me when you are ready to leave."

"Okay, I will."

CHAPTER SEVENTY FIVE

Mary and Kathy waited at the passenger gate at Baltimore-Washington International Airport. They watched the airplane from Cheyenne land and pull into the dock for unloading. Airport workers scurried below to unload the baggage onto a small truck. They waited anxiously as the passengers filed down the gate corridor.

Don eventually appeared with a small travel bag in his hand. He still looked thinner but much better than months before. A light brown full beard framed his face. Kathy ran over first.

"Donny, Donny," she said as she wiped tears of joy from her face.

She hugged him so hard, he winced in pain. Mary went over and joined in.

"I can't believe it's you," Kathy said as she stared at his face.

"We tried so hard to find you and we were so worried and frustrated and when we couldn't."

Don held them smiling with tears in his eyes, not finding the words to say anything.

"Were going back to Salisbury," Mary explained.

"I have the den all ready. Molly will be excited to see you."

"Great," Don finally said as he followed them out.

On the trip from BWI to Salisbury, Kathy and Mary had many questions about the events leading up to Don's disappearance. Don regaled his harrowing experiences after Marna's death. After he thought that he killed Blackman, he did not want the police to connect him to the murder. He explained that the dangerous people employed by Simms could have been a threat to them as they were to him. He feared for his life. He was pursued in New York, Springfield, and later, in Wyoming. That's when he left his van on the exit.

"Donny, we got a call from the sheriff that they had found your remains on the prairie," Kathy said sadly.

From the front passenger's seat, Don looked out the windshield and not at Kathy. Then he turned toward her.

"Kathy, I had to make them think I was dead."

"They came to the trailer that I was staying at looking for me. I don't know how they found the place, but they shot the guy who lived there. I took his truck and planted the body out on the prairie with my coat, clothes and identification on it. Since we had basically the same build, eye and hair color, I thought they wouldn't be able to tell the difference by the time they found the body. Don't you see...I had to convince them that I was dead so they would stop looking for me. I couldn't tell you about any of it."

Kathy looked at him in disbelief. This was the most bizarre story she had ever heard.

"It must have worked because they left me alone."

"I'm glad they did."

Don was safe and alive that's what mattered to her.

CHAPTER SEVENTY SIX

At last, they entered the town of Salisbury. Mary drove down the street and parked in front of the house. Don just sat and looked at it for a minute. He couldn't believe he was there.

As they entered the front door, Molly bolted out of the kitchen and jumped with her front paws on Don's stomach and with her tail wagging vigorously, raising her head towards him as he petted her. They had dinner, a joyful one, with everyone smiling.

Afterwards, they sat in the living room. Mary and Don were on the sofa and Kathy sat in the stuffed chair next to it. With Molly sitting next to him, Don was thoughtfully quiet as he stroked her head.

"There is something I haven't told you about."

The two women looked at him quizzically, not expecting there could be more than they had already learned.

Don paused for a moment.

"I'm an addict."

Looking stunned, Mary said, "an addict?"

"Yes mom… My use of pain medication after my accident got out of control. My excuse was my back pain and I didn't realize how out of control it was getting. I began drinking heavily too…. I just couldn't deal with Marna's death. I needed to escape. As he looked down at the floor, tears formed in Don's eyes as his voice choked out the words. I'm sorry I didn't tell either of you… I was so ashamed."

He looked over at his mother longingly, hoping for forgiveness. She went over to the sofa and joined Kathy to hug him. They were so glad he was alive. Any multitude of sins would not diminish that.

Taking in his families love and allowing his guilt to diminish; Don sat there a few minutes before speaking.

"I'm clean and sober now. I started going to meetings in Jackson to keep me on the right path."

"We're glad. Kathy said."

"We are also glad you are here," Mary added.

It was late. After a big day, Mary had gone to bed.

Don and Kathy sat together across from the fireplace in the living room with Molly curled up on her bed sleeping.

Kathy sat in silence for a few moments reflecting on her experience of searching for her brother.

"You know, I found your briefcase."

"You did!"

"Yeah, you left it at the Wyoming State Museum."

"I did? I couldn't remember where I had left it I was so preoccupied. When I realized it was gone, I didn't know where to look for it."

"There were some interesting items inside."

"Do you mean the letter?"

"Yes …it looks like it was written by a Mary S. to Mrs. Lincoln."

"I found that at the archives of the Lincoln Library in Springfield. It is proof that Mary Saratt knew Mary Lincoln"

"Yeah, so… it was signed Mary S. That doesn't mean that it was Mary Saratt."

"That may be true, but the D.C. boardinghouse record I found had an example of her handwriting which matches the handwriting in the letter. The precise formation of the letters in her handwriting reflects a Catholic school education which Mary had in Virginia."

"Why didn't she sign her last name?"

"She did not want to put her full name in writing right then. This was probably the first of several letters. As far as we know, none of those were ever found. Having signed Mary S., it was missed by historians and remained an anonymous letter for all these years.

"Don't you see, Mrs. Lincoln most likely knew about the kidnapping. The letter was written six months before."

"But you don't think she knew about the assassination."

"No. She would have surely told him."

"So have you changed your mind about Mary Saratt being completely innocent?" Kathy said mockingly.

Don smiled back at her.

"I guess I was wrong. This evidence shows she at least had a role in the kidnapping. That would explain why witnesses placed the planning of the kidnapping at her boarding house in D.C. and the items connected to the kidnapping were left at her Sarattsville home."

"What about the copies of the purchase records?"

"I found those ledgers at the National Archives. The expenses of the White House were recorded in them. According to the records, the Lincolns had purchased camphorated opium tincture, which had morphine as its main ingredient. Her son, Willie died less than a year after her husband's presidential inauguration. She had also lost her second child, Tad to typhoid. She had grieved deeply for years. At the time, this was a pretty standard medication for depressed mood as well as for other generalized aliments such as diarrhea and pain. The records also show that a few years later, she purchased several amounts of cocaine elixir. At the time, there was little known about cocaine. Mrs. Lincoln was susceptible to the side effects of these drugs."

"What side effects?"

"Mood swings and hallucinations."

"So she was unstable…not in her right mind."

"Yes, she was unstable. In fact, the president wondered about her and told her that he was worried that she may have to be hospitalized."

"So your theory is that she conspired to kidnap her husband because she was unstable?"

"In addition to her deepening depression, Mary was always highly emotional. She had been that way throughout her marriage to Abe. She was terribly lonely during his many trips. As a political figure and in recent years as president, he was often away. They had become more and more distant. Mary also believed that the ordeal of the war had taken a terrible toll on him and that he too was suffering. In her mind, she hoped that a kidnapping scare might convince him to give up the presidency. She thought that her husband would be released and return to her unharmed and they could resume a normal life."

"Yeah, but what about the military tribunal? Wouldn't federal investigators uncover some evidence that she knew?"

"Kathy, that is possible, but I think that if they uncovered anything, they would overlook any evidence in order to protect the Lincoln family's good name."

"Your theory is very interesting. So… have you started your book?"

"I have written an outline and have started to write the beginning chapters. After I return to New York and have cleared up some unfinished matters, I will resume writing."

CHAPTER SEVENTY SEVEN

After two weeks in Salisbury, Don returned to New York to turn himself in and to confess his role in his assault of Dan Blackman.

Don drove his compact rental car directly to NYPD headquarters from the Marriot Hotel where he was staying. He found the Homicide Department where he had met Detective Sanderson many months before. Sanderson came out into the squad room to meet Don and shook hands with him.

"This is my partner, Detective Levering."

Don reached towards her, smiled and they shook hands.

He gave Sanderson a serious look and got to the point. "Detective, you know why I am here. I am responsible for Dan Blackman's injuries. I honestly thought that I had killed him."

"Mr. Kendall, I'm glad that you have come in to clear this up—but you will have to check in with the New Jersey State Police since it happened there."

"I thought that I might have to Detective, but it felt more comfortable talking to you since we already knew each other from Marna's murder case."

"You were missing for a long time. Why did you decide to come back to New York to turn yourself in?" Sanderson wondered.

"I felt guilty for running. I realize now that it was a mistake and I am willing to take responsibility for it. It is not an excuse, but I was being chased by John Weaver and his buddies. I know that you are aware of that."

"Yes I am, but Mr. Kendall, you are still in a lot of trouble. Committing assault and fleeing the scene is quite serious."

"I know Detective. I just want to live normally again—without fear."

"That is honorable," Levering commented.

"Lucky for you that Blackman lived," Sanderson remarked. "He was in a coma for a month. Why did you injure him anyway?"

"We were involved in a fist fight. He tried to punch me and I fought back. He fell and hit his head. I panicked and ran. I thought that I looked pretty guilty."

"Running is never a solution…but you may have a case for self defense," Levering surmised.

"Why did you go to his apartment?"

"I was trying to get information about Marna's murder."

Sanderson chimed in. "You mean Marna Anderson. Judith Depetro confessed to it," he said smiling.

Don looked at Sanderson in disbelief.

"Judith…Why?"

"She was jealous of your relationship."

"She was always such a good friend. I had no idea."

Trying to comprehend this revelation, Don paused.

"I read about the insider trading convictions and the other charges. How did you find out?"

"Dan Blackman was instrumental in helping us make the connection. Matthew Simms was offered a deal to testify that he hired the security firm to harass you and Ms. Anderson. As part of the deal he helped us find Weaver."

"Weaver continued to follow me out to Wyoming. He and his men were responsible for killing a guy named Matt Daniels, the owner of a trailer I was hiding at."

"He can still be charged in that crime. The authorities in that jurisdiction have to handle it."

CHAPTER SEVENTY EIGHT

As a result of Dan Blackman pressing charges and Don turning himself in, he was charged with first degree assault. He appeared before a judge in the Essex County Circuit Court in New Jersey. He was placed on bail until his hearing a month later.

Don had hired an attorney to represent him, George Ripley. George was a short man with a receding hair line, a brown mustache and a perpetually reddened face making it difficult to determine if he was embarrassed about something or was sunburned.

When the trial date arrived, George was well prepared. He had told Don that the sentencing guidelines were from five to ten years in prison and that they had a good chance to get a light sentence if they could prove it was self defense and make the case that he came forward voluntarily.

The court room, located in a larger complex of offices for various public servants, was small. It seated fifty people. There was a smattering of people in the courtroom, most of whom filled the front portion of seats.

Although close to a larger metropolitan area, it was in a suburban jurisdiction. Crime was not the norm. As a rule, there were not a large number of felony cases.

Don and George were seated at the defendant's table to the left of the room facing the judge's bench with The United States and New Jersey flags posted behind it. The prosecutor was opposite them on the right. His graying temples and stanch demeanor exuded experience and professionalism.

The clerk announced, "All rise," as the judge came into the courtroom and sat down. He was a young man for a judge—about forty-five, tall, thin with a slender face and a long nose. His brown hair was short, parted on the right and neatly trimmed.

Ready to get started, he wasted no time.

"Mr. Kendall you are charged with first degree assault. How to you plead?"

Don looked at George for a second. "Not guilty, your honor. It was in self defense."

The prosecutor interjected. "Your honor, the state will establish that Mr. Kendall caused significant harm to the plaintiff and fled the scene. There are witnesses who will establish this."

"We can decide that at the proper time, the judge stated. Your plea of not guilty is entered into the record Mr. Kendall."

The prosecutor called his first witness, Dan Blackman.

Blackman slowly walked from his seat in the gallery down the isle to the witness stand to the right of the judge to be was sworn in. He stepped up and sat down in the witness stand. The prosecutor walked up and looked at Blackman.

"Mr. Blackman, was Donald Kendall at your apartment in the Falstaff apartment complex on October third, nineteen seventy-seven?"

"Yeth he was," Blackman said with a mild lisp.

"What happened that day?"

"Don Kendall barged into my apartment demanding to know about a man he thought killed his girlfriend. I didn't like it. We began fighting and he tackled me. I fell into my coffee table and hit the thide of my head."

"Will you point out the man who you are referring to?" Blackman pointed to Don.

"Let the record show that the witness identified Mr. Kendall."

"What injuries did you sustain in that fall?"

"I was knocked unconscious and my skull was cracked on the right thide. There was extensive bleeding. Due to the head trauma, I was in a coma for a month."

"Would it be fair to say that you are lucky to be alive?"

"Yeth," Blackman said staring directly at Don.

"Are there any present difficulties due to the injury?"

Blackman looked angrily at Don. "My face is paralyzed due to nerve damage on the right thide."

"Mr. Blackman, did Mr. Kendall try to help you after you fell?"

George interjected. "Your honor, how can the witness answer that since he was unconscious."

The observers in the gallery unsuccessfully stifled their laughter.

The judge banged his gavel. "Order, order."

The prosecutor continued. "Your honor, the people will establish that Mr. Kendall fled the scene. A witness at the Falstaff Apartment complex observed Mr. Kendall leaving the apartment. I call Lawrence Sanders to the stand."

This witness, who had heard the commotion and had gone to Blackman's apartment, testified that a man fitting Don's description was there and that he fled immediately afterwards.

Don began to worry. This didn't look good. He felt guilty about harming Dan Blackman—he really didn't have to lose his temper and strike him.

Blackman was called back to the stand for cross examination. George got up and approached the witness stand. He looked at Blackman for a moment.

"Mr. Blackman, you testified that you were fighting with Mr. Kendall. Who started it?"

"Kendall started it! Blackman said angrily."

"Isn't it true that you punched Mr. Kendall before he tackled you?"

"I don't remember that."

George looked sternly at the witness. "Mr. Blackman, remember that you are under oath. Did you punch my client first?"

"Well...I may have, but he had no right to attack me like that."

"So, Mr. Kendall responded to your punch to defend himself."

Blackman just looked at him, not answering.

The judge took a recess to deliberate. After an hour, he returned from his chambers to hand down his ruling. All in attendance rose to hear the verdict.

"I rule that Mr. Kendall acted in self defense in attacking Mr. Blackman. However, Mr. Kendall, you did not render assistance to the victim who sustained serious injuries. This is a serious matter and cannot be condoned. Mr. Kendall, taking into account that you have no previous criminal record, and that you have surrendered yourself to face the charges, I find you guilty of second degree assault. You will receive probation before judgment for two years. During your probationary period, Mr. Kendall, if you have any further charges, it will be a violation of your probation and you will be imprisoned for a period of four years."

The judge adjourned court, struck his gavel, and exited the courtroom.

Don sighed in relief and shook hands with George. The trial was over. This was the best outcome he could have hoped for.

Now that this was over, he wanted to return to Wyoming and press charges against the men who had attempted to kill him, and had gunned down Matt Daniels. In order to do this, he was going to have to admit to moving the body and leaving his identification. Now, he wanted to question Weaver himself to find out the names of the other men.

Sanderson had told him that after he was convicted, Weaver was sent to Rikers Island Prison in New York.

CHAPTER SEVENTY NINE

The next day, Don drove to Rikers Island from the Marriott Hotel. The island was in the East River between Queens and the mainland of the Bronx.

It was a sunny autumn day. The sun glistened and reflected on the windshield as he passed patches of trees next to housing developments and apartment complexes. The island came into view as he crossed over the Francis Buono Bridge.

Don began to think about Carol. It had been a long time since he had been in a relationship. He decided that, now that he was back, he would call her. She might possibly be involved with someone else by now, or perhaps over the time that had elapsed since they were together, she may no longer had feelings for him. Regardless, he was going to give it a try.

As he crossed into the huge complex a security gate came into view. He pulled up, stated that he was a visitor, and inquired about the location of the main building. He showed his identification and was waived in.

The Otis Bantum Correctional Center housed the detained male adults. As he entered the front area, two guards stood at a metal detector preceded by a conveyer belt. Don emptied his pockets, took off his watch and placed the items into a square plastic container. One of the security guards scanned his body with a metal detector wand. He was told to pass through and the guard gave him a visitor's pass to clip on his jacket.

Don found the reception office and inquired at the desk. Weaver's name was listed as an inmate at that part of the facility. He was escorted to the visitor's area by another guard. It was a large room with tables and chairs. People of different descriptions sat waiting for their turn to see the inmates.

In an adjoining room were ten privacy booths. A thin sheet metal wall separated them and a thick Plexiglas wall separated the visitors from the prisoners. A black telephone was mounted on the wall of each side.

Don sat in one of the empty booths facing the Plexiglas. Weaver walked in on the other side with a surprised look on his face. He sat down in the chair across from Don. They both picked up the telephones from their cradles.

"I thought you were dead," Weaver said into his phone.

His normally primped blond hair looked as if he was having a bad hair day. His face looked haggard and bags had formed under his eyes, the cyst more pronounced.

Don was struggling to control his anger. This man had made his life hell. He needed the information he came for and would not get it if he went off on him.

Weaver had a puzzled look on his face.

"How did you get here?"

"You did your best to get rid of me…but I'm a survivor," Don said, smiling calmly.

Weaver looked around for eaves droppers. "We shot you in that trailer park."

"You shot the wrong guy. He owned the trailer I was staying at. Did you actually think you had killed me?"

"Yeah…that guy really looked like you."

"So you stopped looking for me after that?" Don was disappointed that he had gone to such lengths to deceive them. It had all been for nothing. He had to forget that and find out who Weaver's accomplices were.

Who do you mean… we?"

"Russell and another guy."

"Russell?"

"Yeah, I hired Russell James to help me find you."

"Who else was there?"

"I'm not saying anymore. I am already in enough trouble. I'll be in here for twenty-five years."

Don was becoming impatient but had to keep his cool.

"Do you have any idea what you put me through? You beat up my girlfriend, shot at me on Long Island and followed me after I got to Wyoming… I'm curious, how did you know I was going there?"

Weaver smiled with twisted satisfaction. He was beginning to enjoy this conversation.

"Dan Blackman told me where you worked. I called there and talked to your secretary."

"Paulette?"

"Yeah. I told her that I was a friend of yours. She told me that you had left the job there and was traveling west following the

Lincoln National Highway. After I researched it, I knew that the monument would be a place that you would stop. It was a matter of when."

"Why did you go to such great lengths?"

"I guess it was a challenge. Besides, I didn't want to end up in jail."

"That didn't work out did it?" Don said sarcastically.

"We thought that you knew too much about the illegal stock trades. At the time, I thought that we had killed your girlfriend." Weaver said, thinking that the water was already under that bridge.

"Did you follow me to Springfield?"

"That's right," Weaver said smugly.

"Did you try to run me off the road and later mess up my room?"

"You guessed it."

"Did anyone help you?"

"Yeah, Sam. He was with me at Marna's apartment, broke into your room for me and later, was on Long Island."

"Do you mean Sam Jenkins?" Don recalled the name from the article in the *New York Times*. He remembered confronting and chasing the stocky man out of his room and, his run in on Long Island with Jenkins and Weaver.

"That's right. We thought that it would scare you off. You are one persistent bastard," he said looking at Don almost admiringly.

CHAPTER EIGHTY

After leaving Rikers Island and getting the answers he needed, his thoughts returned to Carol. He had not seen her since he left his position at Klein. He still felt that if he had given it a chance, the relationship could have blossomed. It was too soon after Marna's death. He began thinking about the time they had spent together. He smiled when he thought about her participation in the séance at the Mary Saratt Museum which seemed like a lifetime ago.

He went back to the Marriot Hotel where he was staying on the Upper East Side. He took the elevator to his room. After entering, Don stopped for a minute after passing a mirror on the wall. Although somewhat thinner, he was beginning to regain a healthy look. His skin was back to its usual color. His beard was neatly trimmed and gave him a distinguished look. He had continued his yoga and meditation since stopping all use of mind altering substances. The back pain nagged him at times but was now much less severe.

Don took out the New York Metro telephone book and sat down in a stuffed chair in the living room. He looked up Dowling and located her phone number at the address he remembered. He picked up the receiver and dialed.

"Hello," Carol said in a phone answering voice.

"Carol… This is Donny."

"Donny!" She said excitedly. It's great to hear from you. I got a call from Kathy after she heard that you were alive and well. We were all so worried. I have really missed you."

"Carol, I have missed you too. Listen, I am back in town. I would like to get together."

"Where are you staying?"

"I'm at the Marriott on East Sixty-Fourth Street."

"You remember where I live don't you?"

"Sure, apartment three-oh-four at the Archstone on Fifty-Fourth."

"You got it. When do you want to come over?"

"How about eight tonight?"

"That sounds wonderful. I will look for you then."

The evening arrived and Don took a cab to Carol's apartment twelve blocks away. He entered the large lobby and took the elevator upstairs. Don took a breath as he knocked on the door. After looking through the peep hole, Carol unlocked the door and opened it. She looked fabulous. She had on a yellow chiffon blouse and navy blue bell bottom slacks. Her light brown hair was pulled back and fell on her shoulders. She rushed through the open door and embraced Don. Surprised, Don wrapped his arms around her, pulling her close to him. Carol took his hand and led him in.

Don looked into Carol's brown eyes. He hadn't realized how much he had missed her. He slipped off his coat and they sat down on the couch.

"Can I offer you something to drink? I have a bottle of wine open or perhaps a scotch."

"No thanks, I don't drink anymore...it's a long story."

"I'm sure that I will hear all about it," Carol said knowingly.

"Carol, how have you been?"

"I have been good. Work is going great."

"Are you seeing anyone?"

"Not at the moment," she teased.

"I met someone about a year ago. We went out a few times but there just weren't any sparks, so I ended it."

"I'm glad," Don said smiling.

"I really didn't give us a chance. I was still missing Marna. You probably thought I was crazy taking you along to that séance in addition to my obsession with Mary Saratt."

"The last time I saw you...you were talking a little crazy... something about going to Wyoming to write your book and being a prophet of men."

Don looked at Carol with a half smile.

"Carol...I had been taking a sleeping medication. Not only that, the experience at the museum affected me profoundly."

Don paused, reflecting on the words.

"Carol. I couldn't tell you that I was leaving town. I'm sorry. I had to leave New York because I thought I had killed someone defending myself in a fight. Thankfully, that's all settled now."

"I didn't know what had happened to you. I thought you had lost interest in seeing me."

"Carol, it's complicated… in addition to the altercation, I had to elude some very bad people. I didn't tell anyone about it until recently. I have to return to Wyoming to take care of some things. When I get back, I want to move back to New York."

"You could stay with me until you find a place."

"I would love that."

Carol embraced Don snuggling his neck.

"I'm glad you are here," she said in his ear.

She led him to the bedroom. They kissed hungrily, their tongues probing. Carol pulled her blouse over her head and Don unhooked her black bra, revealing her voluptuous breasts. Don unbuttoned his shirt threw it to the floor, removed his tee shirt, and pulled himself to her. They held each other and their naked skin touched, further arousing them. They dropped their remaining clothes on the floor and made love.

Afterward, Don lay wrapped in Carol's arms with his face snuggled under her chin. For the first time in years he felt safe and at peace.

CHAPTER EIGHTY ONE

Don drove over the mountainous terrain toward Rawlins after his flight landed in the Laramie Airport. It all looked vaguely familiar to him and brought back unpleasant memories of those harrowing days. He approached Sherman Hill and the top of Lincoln's head appeared as the sculptured memorial came into view. He thought about the injustices he experienced here as he drove over the rise in the terrain and passed the exit. *These bastards aren't going to get away with murder,* Don thought. *I didn't deserve to be threatened, followed and harassed. Matt Daniels didn't deserve to die.*

As he drove, Elk Mountain appeared in the distance. For the first time, he appreciated its majestic beauty—bluish-green, its slopes towering high, capped by snow, as fluffy, white clouds floated above it in a blue sky. As he drove closer, Don saw that on its slopes, an elk lazily grazed.

Don arrived in Rawlins. He checked into his motel and drove his rental car over to the court house. At the sheriff's office, he asked to talk to Sheriff Coburn. He was told that the sheriff was not in and Don agreed to wait for him.

After an hour, the sheriff arrived. As he entered the room, Don stood up to greet him.

"Sheriff Coburn?"

"That's me."

"I'm Don Kendall."

The sheriff looked down trying to remember. "Kendall," he said to himself.

"Oh yeah, Don Kendall."

"I'll be damned. You are alive. Until we found that body on the prairie, I would have sworn that you had gotten a ride out of here. It looks as if I was right.

Coburn got a quizzical look on his face. "Do you know how that body got your I.D. on it?"

"Sheriff, I'm afraid that I had to make people believe I was dead to stay alive myself. I moved the body of Matt Daniels, the man who owned the trailer in Casper and put my clothing and identification on it. The people who killed him were trying to kill me."

"We were looking for Daniels. We thought that after the shooting out there, he had run off."

"Mr. Kendall, it is against the law to tamper with a crime scene, but it sounds like you had a good reason. I can see why you might have feared for your life. We were out there to investigate reports by the neighbors. There was one hell of a fire fight out there. Do you know who the shooters were?"

"Yes I do, which is the reason I wanted to mislead anyone who was looking for me. They were hired to follow me out here from

New York. I am hoping that Carbon County will charge them with attempting to murder me and the murder of Matt Daniels."

Coburn took on a more serious look. "If someone was murdered in my county and you can prove it, I will certainly charge them."

"Sheriff, I was wondering, can you tell me what happened to my van?"

"Van?"

"Yeah, the Chevy Sportvan I dove out here. My sister, Kathy told me that you had moved it out at the rest area. She said that it was broken into and that my address book was missing. I know that I didn't have it. I bailed out of the van and left most everything there. Another thing sheriff, someone apparently used my telephone charge card to make a call from Washington State. I think they stole it from my van."

"Right now, your van is on the impound lot. We never found out who broke in…probably somebody who saw it parked at the rest area and took advantage of an opportunity."

Don wondered if that was really what happened.

"My mother and sister were not very happy with you. They were very frustrated that you did not do more to find me."

"I was within my rights and besides, isn't it your fault that you were missing?" the sheriff said defensively.

"Sheriff, perhaps I misled a lot of people, but it was never what I wanted to happen."

"Okay, if you say so," he said looking at Don judgmentally.

"Would you release the van back to me? I was hoping I could drive it back to New York."

"Sure. It has been sitting in the lot collecting dust. We were going to try and get rid of it anyway."

"Deputy Jones, please take Mr. Kendall's statement."

Coburn went to his office. Jones motioned for Don to come back and sit down at his desk behind the front counter. He sat down and began telling the whole story.

CHAPTER EIGHTY TWO

It had been two years since Don had lived in New York. He missed the place. He said goodbye to his mother and sister in Salisbury and moved some of his possessions in with Carol.

He thought about the ordeal he had endured and took a deep breath. The nightmare was over and he could return to a normal life. What would he do? The book he had wanted to publish had to be finished. Maybe he could work again on Madison Avenue.

John Weaver and Russell James were being charged with attempted murder by the Carbon County Prosecutor's Office. Unfortunately, Don had compromised the crime scene and the autopsy of the body of Matt Daniels was lost, making it impossible to prove his murder. At least they could be charged with their attempt on Don's life. The other man employed by Weaver and shot by Daniels was never identified. He had simply vanished. Don was going to return to Wyoming to testify at the trial in a few weeks.

He walked into the Narcotics Anonymous meeting he had found at the Wesley Methodist Church hall. The Secretary and a speaker sat at the front of the downstairs room. There were twenty people seated in chairs lined up in rows on the linoleum floor. At the front of the room was a cloth banner which listed the twelve steps in red, large letters.

The speaker was a large man who appeared to be about forty years old—his hair graying, his face lined beyond his years. He had on a loose fitting tan sweater from which a thick neck protruded.

"My name is Tom and I'm an addict," he stated.

"Hi Tom," the group said, greeting him.

Tom told his story of his struggle with drug addiction and his new life after recovery. Others began to share their experiences.

Since he had attended A.A. meetings in Wyoming, Don had gotten a foothold in a twelve-step program. In New York he had begun to go to N.A. in addition to the A.A. meetings he was already attending. Although he had attended the group several times, he had never opened up. He had come to this meeting determined that he would tell his story. The Secretary of the meeting asked if anyone else wanted to speak.

Then Don spoke about how his addiction started and how it had changed his life. He then told of his surrender and recovery.

When the meeting came to a close, the group stood in a circle and held hands. Together, they said the Serenity Prayer.

"God grant me serenity
to accept the things I cannot change
the courage to change the things I can
and the wisdom to know the difference."

"It works, work it. Keep coming back!"